TASK FORCE TWO: PACK'S EARTH ANGEL

The Men of Five-O #9

Dixie Lynn Dwyer

LOVEXTREME FOREVER

Siren Publishing, Inc.
www.SirenPublishing.com

A SIREN PUBLISHING BOOK
IMPRINT: LoveXtreme Forever

TASK FORCE TWO: FENNIGAN PACK'S EARTH ANGEL
Copyright © 2014 by Dixie Lynn Dwyer

ISBN: 978-1-63258-380-2

First Printing: December 2014

Cover design by Les Byerley
All art and logo copyright © 2014 by Siren Publishing, Inc.

Printed in the U.S.A.

PUBLISHER
Siren Publishing, Inc.
www.SirenPublishing.com

DEDICATION

Dear Readers,

Thank you for purchasing this legal copy of *Fennigan Pack's Earth Angel*.

May you enjoy the journey of one very strong, independent woman who must come to terms with the magical powers bestowed upon her. As if that isn't enough, she must learn to adapt to being the mate to six Alpha men, while also maintaining that independence, her career, and her intended destiny as the first Earth Angel.

With men as dominating, bossy, and wild as Fennigan pack, this may be the fight of Salina's life, and also a time for change and adaptation, being mated to one sexy, strong-willed detective, for the Fennigan pack men.

Sounds like the recipe for disaster, or maybe the recipe for a powerful love story.

Happy reading.

Hugs!
~Dixie~

TASK FORCE TWO: FENNIGAN PACK'S EARTH ANGEL

The Men of Five-O #9

DIXIE LYNN DWYER
Copyright © 2014

Prologue

Angus missed his brothers. Since losing their mate, Margo, during the great fight between the demon and the Goddesses of the Circle, life just hadn't been the same. He and Quinn were now in the United States instead of their homeland in Ireland. Angus looked down the side street, and his wolf yearned to run free. It felt so captive and held prisoner. It was like he lost part of himself even though he and his brothers hadn't begun the mating bond with Margo. That didn't mean it didn't hurt.

He glanced at Quinn, who sat on the ledge of the building, appearing just as grim as Angus felt. He wondered how the others were doing.

Adrian and Brady, those two crazy, psycho bastards were in the mountains hunting down rogue wolves and attempting to build small armies against smaller packs. They found the jobs to be rewarding and they risked their lives so easily now because there didn't seem to be anything worthwhile to live for. Even their bond as brothers had weakened. Angus took a deep breath and released it.

Delaney and Eagan were in County Clare, Ireland, near Declan Pack, working for the Brothers of Were and ensuring that Were packs were following the new rules and regulations. Lately there had been some resistance, and some packs were initiating takeovers to build up their armies. Delaney and Eagan were enforcing the laws of the Jewel of Ireland and still wading through rogue wolves and packs that weren't compliant with the new laws and regulations set forth by the new leaders of the Circle of Elders.

So many changes, and yet here was Angus, an Alpha, a known warrior of the gods and goddesses, a soldier of the Brothers of Were, and a leader of a task force that had fallen apart.

Was there any reason to go on? Was this life, this sworn testament of revenge he deemed more important than living itself, worth sucking the remainder of the life left inside of him?

He looked out across the city skyline. New York. He'd trailed Vargon Carbarone all the way to fucking New York City, and he still didn't have enough evidence to prove to the Circle that Vargon was the one who killed Margo.

But he was there, and he had help that night. As a multitude of battles took place around the world, good versus evil, the demon versus the goddesses, all others loyal to the Circle joined forces. Margo, a healer, took off without warning to any of them. She called and said it was her destiny and that the goddesses needed her.

He shook his head. They needed her, too. Wolves searched all their lives hoping to find a mate and have the ultimate bond and connection. They had finally gotten their chance at happiness, at a tradition none of them thought they could ever have. Fennigan Pack was no longer whole because of Vargon Carbarone and his associates.

I will avenge Margo's death. I will seek justice for all those you have killed and destroyed. I'm watching you, and when the time comes, I will seek my revenge and bring justice to my family, my brothers, once and for all.

* * * *

Salina "Sal" Santos locked gazes with a set of glowing yellow eyes. It was insane, the feelings that consumed her body. Something clicked inside of her. Something deep, so very deep she felt tears of emotions hit her eyes, and of course she quickly submerged the show of emotion. She was tough, self-sufficient, and distrusting to most everyone except for Reggie, her partner in the police department, and of course, her father, Pierce, her only living relative.

Her dad, Pierce, was a quiet man, retired from law enforcement as well after sustaining injuries from a brutal attack when she was only two years old. Sometimes she thought she remembered the incident, or perhaps envisioned what took place in her mind. She saw scattered bits and pieces, like her mom screaming and covering her face with her hands, and her dad roaring in pain, looking fierce, almost inhuman. But she knew it couldn't be true. He was a man and not some beast. The thought had her swallowing hard as she stared at the yellow eyes in the distance.

Everything else seemed to fade to silence, even the passing cars every now and then on the quiet side street in Queens, New York. The sirens echoed in the distance perhaps blocks and blocks away. Her heart raced, the feelings and desire to run and help, or at least see if she could aid the victims of a crime, a fire, a homicide, entered her mind. But the glowing yellow eyes were so very strong. She stared harder, trying to figure out who they were, or even what they were, for every ounce of her felt as if the person, the thing behind the glowing eyes was evil. She took a few unsteady steps forward, her chest feeling harder, stronger, almost as if something pressed back against it, trying to stop her from investigating the thing in the darkness.

It was like a shield of armor. Was it protecting her, or holding her back from figuring out a truth of some sort? She of course pushed, persisted to move on and challenge the power holding her back.

As she moved, struggled to trudge onward, she felt her breath growing rapid. Her lungs heaved in and out for air like some asthmatic in the middle of an attack.

She was getting closer, weaker with every step, and as she felt her body give out and use the last bit of strength to heave another breath and look upward, she saw its face and screamed out in terror. Teeth, fangs, drool. A monstrous beast growled at her, causing fear like nothing else to consume her body. She fell backward and landed on the pavement as the thing slowly crawled over her.

"You're mine now, Salina. All mine."

Salina awoke with a start. She was gasping for air, her mouth and throat completely dry as she tried to move her tongue and get some sort of moisture there to swallow and breathe. She reached for the bottle of water, relieved that she remembered to keep it there just for this reason. She undid the cap, guzzled down the contents, and felt the panic begin to lessen.

Why do I have this same dream? What does it mean? Why do I feel like it's true, and that this thing does exist?

She pushed herself up from the bed and read the clock. Five a.m. It was time to get up and take a run before work. She would have just enough time if she hurried.

She grabbed her things, brushed her teeth, drank down a breakfast shake, and swallowed her vitamins. She stared out the window that overlooked the back of the town house development and straight to the woods. She wondered if her dreams had to do with her profession? As she put on her sneakers and finished getting ready, she analyzed her dream and what it might mean.

She grabbed her key, placed it into the small zip-up pocket on the back of her Athleta pullover shirt, and headed out the door.

As her feet pounded on the pavement and her breath began to fill with the warm spring air, she thought about her dream.

The darkness, not seeing anything at first and then suddenly the yellow eyes probably has something to do with being a homicide detective. I never know what to expect when I pull up onto a call, a crime scene in the aftereffects of some monster's brutality to another human being, or even multiple. Hence, the beast with the yellow eyes. He must represent the evil killer, the one I search for and seek. My dream always ends the same way, with the beast, the sharp teeth, and the monstrous expression, and the evil darkness that I feel surround me and paralyze me must represent the killers that go free. The ones I can't find and prove that they indeed are the ones responsible for the deaths I investigate. And thoughts of my dad. Well, that just means my subconscious remembers his story of how he was injured during an investigation, and my mom screaming is because of the pain she more than likely sustained from the car accident she died in. Yes, that has to be it. See, Sal, no worries. No worries at all. I'm not losing my mind. I'm just an obsessed workaholic consumed with catching killers and bringing justice to victims' families.

Then why do I feel like there's more? Why does that monster seem so real to me?

Her chest tightened, and she suddenly had the sensation that someone was watching her just as she continued running through the small woods along the dirt path. She looked around her and listened deeply for any sign of presence, animal or human. She didn't like the feeling she had. Something wasn't right. Something was on the horizon coming her way. What it was she didn't know, but whatever it was she felt intimidated, and Salina Santos didn't take well to intimidation. No way, no how.

Chapter 1

Angus and Quinn Fennigan stood by the balcony looking over the city lights of New York. It was getting late, and time to search the streets and follow those two assholes, Luka Carbarone and one of his pack members Centron. Every time Angus thought about the Carbarone Pack, he wanted to kill them all, go rogue himself, and destroy any remnants of them from this realm and all others. But he couldn't. With all the changes in the Circle of Elders still going on, and new members being sworn in, packs combining to gain force and power, it was no use in fighting the council's decision. He just couldn't believe that no one could prove Carbarone was responsible for Margo's death. She was his mate, and his brothers'. Her death had destroyed each of them inside. Now his brothers were scattered around the world, aiding in pack laws, the enforcement of protocol for the new Circle, and being sure to keep order and control. He missed them and so did Quinn.

"So, you take the East Side and I'll take the West Side?" Quinn asked. He looked at his brother and nodded his head. Quinn was just as big as him. Over six feet three, filled with muscles, attitude, and tattoos along their arms and chests. Quinn had blond hair where Angus's hair was dark brown and his eyes were grayer than Quinn's ocean blue.

"I want them to fuck up so badly. I want to be there when they do so we can give it to them," Quinn stated as he gripped the balcony railing and looked out across the city. They tried so hard to fit in here in New York. Their thick Irish brogues gained them more attention than they were used to in Ireland. Most people, especially women, found it appealing. They had some wild times together, had their share of women, trying to get the fact that they lost their mate out of their minds despite the fact that they never had the chance to make love to Margo and bind to her. It was horrible. He'd failed his mate, he'd failed his brothers, and once Angus killed the Carbarone responsible for murdering his mate, he could end his own life and let his brothers move on without him. He had failed as their Alpha and as their brother and leader.

He felt the hand on his shoulder and then heard Quinn's voice.

"You did not fail us or Margo. The gods have the final say in life and what transpires. Don't you know that? Killing yourself will do nothing but cause me, Adrian, Brady, Delaney, and Eagan to suffer more. Don't be ridiculous." Quinn then glanced out at the city. "Look out there, brother. There is more to life than what we've had to deal with thus far. You'll see. We'll get our revenge and then we'll move on. If the council finds fault in our actions, then so be it. We step down from our place in the Brothers of Were, as Alpha rulers to the Goddesses of the Circle, and we live the rest of our lives in seclusion off the land. At least we'll be together, and we won't be susceptible to any more pain."

Angus thought about that as he stepped back and cleared his throat. "Let's do what needs to be done. I don't like the feelings I've been having lately. It's like despite all the changes, good changes in the Circle and with the goddesses being revealed, there's still more evil out there, and more attempts at taking over the good."

"That's because there are. It's been quiet for the most part, but I feel it, too. I feel it stronger since arriving in New York. Let's get ready to go, and open our wolf spirits to the directions of the gods and goddesses. For they know our destiny, and they will guide us."

"Good luck and be safe. Call me if you spot them and I will get to you," Angus told Quinn.

"Same here. No heroics on your own. I would like a piece of them myself," Quinn said then winked.

Angus watched him go and then he grabbed his gun and followed. Tonight there was an edge of trouble on the heels of the soft breeze. His wolf felt it. His spirit felt it. But he was ready. Angus Fennigan didn't care if he lived or died, just as long as he brought justice to his mate once and for all.

* * * *

Salina tried to calm her heavy breathing. She gripped her revolver in her hands, feeling the cold, hard metal embed against her skin. She was trying not to shake. She needed to maintain control of the situation she was in. She tried to swallow, but her dry, nervous throat nearly made her cough. She couldn't do that. That would alert the creeps that she was in the vicinity.

She cursed Reggie, her partner, for the third time since he took off all gung ho after two guys he spotted and obviously recognized as criminals. Basic training enforced the rule of sticking together and never leaving your partner. But no. Not Reggie. A detective sergeant, her training officer and then partner, for the last five years, and he does this?

She peeked around the corner, keeping her cheek against the concrete wall. It was an old building, by the way the paint peeled away in shredded curls from the walls. It was probably filled with lead paint or even asbestos.

She could hardly make out the scene around the dark corner. Her heart hammered in her chest. Her lungs filled with the damp, moldy smell of old, dilapidated building. She'd called in for backup minutes ago. Why wasn't anyone coming to help? She saw one asshole, his gun pointed to the back of Reggie's head. Somehow, he'd gotten the upper hand on her partner. Another one stood there looking beaten and about to pass out. She felt proud of Reggie. He obviously did some damage to that guy.

She thought she heard a low growl, but looking around her, into the darkness, nothing came into view.

That was all she would need now, some rabid dog coming in and attacking her before she could help Reggie.

"You think you're so fucking smart, pig. You don't know who you're messing with. You don't even know who I am," the gunman stated in a thick Irish accent, his hand steady as he pressed the gun against Reggie's head, giving it a shove.

"Fuck you. I know who you are. You come from a family of shit, your father included!" Reggie yelled back.

Shit, Reggie, don't egg him on. This kid has killed before. It was obvious by the way he held the gun and didn't shake. His expression was cocky, arrogant, and all punk. *How the hell do you know him? Shit, I need to get in there, but if I move now, he'll take the shot and kill Reggie.*

"Fuck you, Fennigan, and your whole fucking bloodline of weak beasts. The clan should have destroyed you all by now. Your pack means shit."

The gunman slammed the barrel of the gun against Reggie's head. Reggie fell over.

Pack? Clan? What the hell?

"Stop, police!" she yelled out. Reggie looked to the side, right at her. His eyes looked funny. They almost glowed yellow. Something made her hesitate and think of the beast in her dream. Then she heard the kid with the gun growl, and when she looked at him, she could have sworn he had sharp teeth. He aimed and fired. Salina didn't hesitate. She took the shot, hitting the gunman with the face of a teenager right in the forehead. She felt the hit to her upper arm, but she turned to the left where the other guy pulled a gun from his hip and pointed it at Reggie. It happened so fast. Two shots rang out. The guy shot Reggie, then turned to shoot her, but she pulled the trigger, hitting him in the forehead. She was an excellent marksman, thanks to her father.

She pulled the radio from her hip.

"Officer down. I repeat, officer down." She gave their location again, demanding to know where the hell their backup was.

She fell to the ground next to Reggie, feeling her own arm ache from the bullet wound. Even if the guy shot further to the right she would be okay. She wore a bulletproof vest.

"Reggie. Reggie, are you okay?" she asked. She heard him chuckling, eyes closed, his breathing funny.

"Reggie?" She didn't know why he didn't answer as she heard sirens in the distance, coming from outside the building as she painstakingly ran her palms along his body where the bullet went.

"You crazy son of a bitch. Holy shit, I love you, Sal. You have got to be the best shot in the department. Whoo!" he yelled out. She gave his shoulder a smack and he cringed.

"I thought he got you. What the fuck, Reggie?"

When she tried to stand up, she felt dizzy. He reached for her. "Slow down there, cowgirl. The adrenaline rush is leaving your body. Just sit still." He tried to sit up, but he cringed then moaned and groaned.

"Fuck, I don't remember it hurting this fucking bad," he said, referring to being shot even with a bulletproof vest on.

She chuckled this time. "Serves you right. Why the fuck did you run off like that? We're partners. We're supposed to stick together. You didn't know if there were other people in here. People that could help them. How did you know that kid anyway? You said something about his father."

"A thank-you would be sufficient."

"A thank-you for what?"

"For saving your ass from getting shot."

"Uh, I did get shot. Which is why I'm bleeding like a fucking fiend right now and feeling dizzy."

He scrunched his eyes together in an expression of concern. He looked at her arm. "Apply pressure to the wound. Shit."

"I am, and I'm fine."

"Fuck, you're not. You got shot. Fuck," he exclaimed, suddenly acting awfully concerned and not so humored by the situation.

He ran his fingers through his salt-and-pepper hair he kept too long. The sexy bachelor loved the attention it got him from the ladies. She shook her head.

"You need an ambulance."

"You need a shrink," she replied.

He stared at her, mouth gaped open, and then he chuckled.

Their backup arrived, better late than never, with guns drawn and calling out, "Police!"

"It's all over. She needs an ambulance," Reggie said and then ran his fingers through his hair, a habit he did when he was concerned. He had a good fifteen years on her, but he was a great partner. As detectives they'd worked on hundreds of cases together. He knew her father, Pierce, and promised him that he would take good care of her. But it seemed that Salina was taking care of Reggie and his wild, old-school ways.

He reached out to her as she was looking down at her arm. He caressed her cheek.

"You did amazing, Sal. Like always. Your dad is going to be pissed off at you for being so gung ho."

"No, he won't. He'll be pissed off at you, for causing me to get shot."

He chuckled as the paramedics arrived and other officers came onto the scene.

"Would one of you like to explain this fucking mess?" their lieutenant asked as he approached, looking around at the two dead bodies with bullet wounds to their foreheads. He sniffed the air and she assumed he was taken aback by the stench of mold and old-building smell.

"Don't look at me. Sal is the one with the sniper shot abilities."

Salina shook her head at her partner.

"Sal, are you okay?" the lieutenant asked. Benjamin McCallister was an older, attractive man, and had a thing for her. She heard Reggie exhale in annoyance as Benjamin placed his hand on her shoulder and looked at her wound.

"Get the fuck over here. This detective's been shot."

"I'm okay, Lieutenant."

He gave her a serious expression. "You've been shot, Sal. Damn. We'll get you looked at immediately." He yelled again as the paramedics entered the room.

"Holy shit. Was that your handiwork, Reggie?" the paramedic asked. Reggie shook his head as he slowly undid the bulletproof vest in obvious pain, scrunching his eyes together. "That's Sal's handiwork."

The paramedic began to undo Salina's shirt to help see where the bullet was. The lieutenant helped to remove her bulletproof vest, and thank God she wore a tank top beneath it, or he would be removing her blouse and she would be sitting here with only a bra on.

She heard a whistle as another two detectives entered the room.

"Hot damn, we've got good timing. I've always wondered what Sal looked like under all those neck-high blouses and slim-fitting dress pants," London Perez said, walking around the front of her to get a better look.

The paramedic chuckled. "Shit, Salina, it's a bad one, but at least the bullet went right through. I'll patch this up best I can and bring you in," he stated as someone yelled about bringing in a gurney. The other paramedic looked at Reggie, who now had his shirt off. She couldn't see any bruising on his stomach or chest. She wondered why. He should be bruised up and red despite the vest protecting him.

Benjamin nudged her arm as the others brought in the gurney.

"No gurney for me. I'm walking out of here," she said firmly.

The paramedic wrapped up her arm, the blood seeping through despite his efforts. She went to stand up and the lieutenant and London reached for her.

"I'm okay," she said, but truth was, she felt awfully dizzy. She leaned in to the lieutenant. His arm went around her waist, his palm landing over her tight abs. She felt uncomfortable, and the way he caressed her, she knew he was taking advantage of the situation. She wished she had some sort of attraction to him, to any man for that matter. But she never felt anything more than a tingling sensation. Now wasn't any different. Besides, she was no damsel in distress. She was a New York City homicide detective. She kicked ass and took names. Fuck being vulnerable and showing weakness.

"I've got you, Sal," Benjamin whispered.

"I'm okay," she replied, trying to stand alone.

"I do, too," London added, placing his hand on her waist on the other side and guiding her along with the lieutenant. Reggie chuckled and she looked at him and gave him the evil eye. Reggie was enjoying this. She got hit on all the time at work but never dated a fellow cop. She didn't want the hassle or the gossip. Plus, if things didn't work out, she would be dragged through the mud. She knew guys, and they could get pretty damn nasty when a woman broke things off with them. It was safer being alone. Who had time for dating or even a love affair anyway?

As they escorted her out of the building to the awaiting ambulance, she saw a crowd had gathered. Considering it was late at night, there were an awful lot of people out here. She scanned the faces out of force of habit. Even though the criminals were dead, she still looked around as if more were watching.

She felt her eyes begin to lose focus when she locked gazes with one very large, dark-haired man. He was gorgeous, and immediately her heart reacted to seeing him. She tried to focus better, losing him for a moment as they lifted her up into the ambulance. When she glanced back, she saw his glowing eyes. She blinked. She felt her body tingle and her pussy ache. *How odd.*

No, it couldn't be. I must be losing my mind.

Salina lay back onto the gurney and the paramedics strapped her in. She closed her eyes, prepared to head to the hospital, but all she saw was his image. The man in black, dark hair, gorgeous face, and glowing eyes. How the hell could his eyes be glowing? She thought about the scene in the building and the teen with the long, sharp teeth. Had she imagined that, too?

"Sal, are you feeling okay?" the paramedic asked her.

She closed her eyes and blinked them again and again. "I think I'm hallucinating," she said.

He smiled. "You're going to be fine. Just rest, and we'll have you in the ER in no time."

She tried to do just that, but then she felt a warm sensation encase her body as she thought about the man in the crowd until she passed out.

Chapter 2

"You crazy bastard. You think they're dead, do you now? You egged them on, and now they want you and they'll want that pretty brunette you've been trying to keep safe. Tell me what the fuck you were thinking?" Jimmy Lannigan, a member of Fagan Pack, asked Reggie Fennigan in his thick Irish brogue.

Reggie ran his fingers through his hair.

"I was focused on bringing those half-vampire scoundrels down. As members of the Carbarone family, it was a sure way to get revenge for what they did to my family. To our family, Jimmy. Those fuckers are the ones who killed Margo, our cousins' mate. They had a hand in the murders we're investigating."

"Yeah, well, Fennigan Pack is aware of what took place here in the States. Two of them are here. Angus and Quinn were following Luka and Centron. They seek their own revenge for the men who killed their mate. Their brothers are scattered all over the world. They haven't been the same since her death. You know you just pulled that partner of yours into the middle of a Were situation. She's human. This isn't good at all."

"I know. I'll protect Sal, and she's pretty damn tough. I want to help my cousins heal, I do. I saw an opportunity and I took it."

"I understand, but our cousins, Fagan Pack along with their mate, Dani, the Declan brothers, and Ava, are not pleased about this occurrence. Declan Pack believes that Carbarone is up to something. Your partner, a human, shot two highly evil relatives to Carbarone. She now has a bull's-eye on her forehead, thanks to you, which means we need to provide some serious protection."

"I've got her covered. I also have some of our pack members surrounding her condo right now."

"That's not enough. Quinn was at the scene yesterday. He said there were other members of Carbarone's family in the vicinity. They've already taken notice to your partner, Sal. Such an odd name for such a strikingly gorgeous woman. Too bad she wasn't a supernatural like a wolf. Then she might just be able to take care of herself."

Reggie swallowed hard. Little did his cousin or the Fennigan or Fagan Packs know that Sal was indeed quite special. She just didn't know it. She could possibly be more powerful than a healer, like Margo, or a foreseer, like Dani. He swallowed hard.

"What are you hiding?"

"Me? I'm not hiding anything. Why would you ask me that?" Reggie asked. He looked around them, being sure no one was taking notice of them talking.

"You know something. I'm your cousin. You better share with me any info that could bring down Margo's killers."

"Jimmy, you do your job and I'll do mine. You can tell Quinn and Angus where to find me."

"They know where you are. Angus was in the crowd the other night. I told you he was tracking Carbarone's men."

"Well then, tell him he and Quinn are more than welcome to join me for dinner tonight. We can discuss the current situation."

"You need to watch over your partner, or the next dead body to turn up and give our packs unwanted attention by the human police will be hers."

Jimmy turned around and left. Reggie took a deep breath and released it. He needed to talk with Sal's dad. This situation had just gotten a hell of a lot worse because he'd decided to allow revenge to rule his wolf mind instead of focusing on protecting Sal. Pierce Santos was going to really give it to him. Reggie thought about his job and the reason he was stationed in the department from the start fifteen years ago. He had a job to do. He was to ensure that the supernatural weren't the ones killing people for fun or just because they needed to feed. He was part of a major organization that was being revamped since the goddesses took over the Circle. He could help run this organization if he didn't keep screwing things up.

In fact, he felt that Sal, if she were a bit more than just human, could be a definite asset to the project. He hoped that he didn't just jeopardize his opportunity to become part of the new organization and special crimes unit.

Damn. I really need to get my shit together.

* * * *

Angus, Alpha leader to Task Force Two, Fennigan Pack, stood by the bar along with his brother Quinn. They stood out like always, and not just because of their Irish brogues. But this was a safe location to meet their cousin Reggie. He looked at Quinn. Blond hair, blue eyes, and such a serious expression it nearly matched Angus's. The rest of their brothers were spread out the last month or so helping to train pack warriors and keep the investigation into underground rogue packs under control. Six months ago they were so angry and distraught about their mate being murdered that there was no talking to them. They wouldn't take orders but then the higher command initiated their own demands. The Goddesses of the Circle revealed themselves, and the Were community united to fight off the ultimate evil. Now it was back to securing the world, and the civilians who had yet to know of the existence of supernaturals.

"What's taking him so long?" Quinn asked, drinking his mug of beer. He would love to visit the Irish bar across town, best known to cater to the Irish clan of Were to make them feel right at home as if in Ireland, but it was too dangerous. Too many mixes of Were, vampire, and fairy filtered through the joint. Too many members of Carbarone's kind, and Angus knew he would lose control. If he had his way, he'd take out all fifty thousand of them, destroying any chances of Carbarone's pack to exist again. But The Goddess wouldn't let him. Not the elders, not Samantha nor Lord Crespin, no one. It seemed to him that something else was occurring, and since he didn't care if he lived or died, he'd attack the situation head-on. When a wolf lost his mate, life just didn't seem worth living anymore.

"He'll be here. He's probably checking on his partner first. Jimmy said that Reggie had her place covered for extra security."

Quinn snorted. "She'll need it. She's as good as dead, you know that, right?"

"I know she tried taking out Luka and Centron, but being of their kind, and obviously having some connections to magic or perhaps a healer, they're already back on the streets. A regular bullet can't kill them, even when shot in the head."

"Hopefully we get the chance to rip their fucking throats out. That ought to do the trick," Quinn said in his thick Irish brogue.

Just then Angus spotted Reggie, and he looked grim. They gave him a hug hello. His salt-and-pepper hair made him mix in as a human aging as the years went on, but soon he would have to relocate, let his natural hair grow, and start the cycle again. Wolves just didn't age, but playing a role in front of humans was important.

"Glad you survived the situation even though you shouldn't have pursued them," Angus told Reggie.

Reggie raised his hands up. "I know I fucked up, but I was thinking about you guys, your brothers, and the shit you've gone through. I saw the opportunity and I took it."

"You're not trained like we are. You never went through the process. You both could have been killed and explaining the human loss would have caused a lot of paperwork to say the least," Quinn said and gave Reggie the once-over.

"I know, I know. I heard it all from Jimmy. So what's the next step? Are you guys still trying to organize a hit on Carbarone?"

"A hit? What the fuck are you talking about?"

"Oh, come on. Are you to going to stand there and try to tell me that you're not ready to pursue Carbarone and his men when you know they're here in the city? We can take them down and destroy their operation. As a matter of fact, I think they're also responsible for the double murder Sal and I are currently investigating."

"What operation would that be?" Angus asked, now crossing his arms in front of his chest. Truth was, as much as he and his brothers would love to kill and destroy Carbarone and his team of criminals, he couldn't. Not unless there was just cause, evidence, and an approval by a higher-up. With the new leaders of the Circle in position, there was a process to go through. From Ava and Dani, it seemed that Carbarone and his associates were on a watch list. No one was able to prove that Carbarone killed Margo, but Fennigan Pack knew. Margo had been going to see an informant and support the bringing down some rogue wolves who were assisting the Goddesses of Love, Were, and Unity when she was killed. A part of them died that day as well.

"The Carbarones are running a series of businesses from loan-sharking to drugs and prostitution. There also seems to be some special abilities from someone aiding them. How else would Luka and Centron had survived the bullets to their heads?"

"We have our orders. You have your cousin. Might I suggest we stop wasting time talking about what already happened and figure out how we're going to keep your human partner alive?" Angus asked.

Reggie looked at them and sighed. "She's an amazing woman. I have known her father for quite some time. I would do anything to keep her safe. Since you know more about Carbarone, what would you suggest I do to ensure her safety?"

"Take her out of here and into hiding," Quinn said and smirked.

"Really? Come one now. You don't know Sal. She's a fighter, and she doesn't back down from shit."

"Yeah, she's pretty good with a gun," Angus stated.

"She's fucking incredible with a gun," Reggie added.

"Well, regular bullets don't do shit to most mystical creatures," Quinn added.

"I was thinking of switching her bullets to silver ones. That way she'd have a fighting chance," Reggie said, sounding very serious.

"She's a human woman. She's weak in comparison to our kind. She won't make it. We'll work on things on our end and see if we can secure grounds for eliminating Carbarone and his associates," Angus stated firmly.

"Like killing your mate who was helping the goddesses isn't enough grounds for elimination?" Reggie asked.

"We've got a new Circle of Elders who want to clean house quietly and carefully. There are changes occurring all across the world. That means they weigh the circumstance by the intensity of the person's crimes. Since Carbarone is capitalizing on humanity's need for consumption of sex and drugs, it doesn't quite fall into termination," Quinn stated in disgust.

"That will eventually change the more they allow such leniency amongst the criminal magical creatures. You'll see."

"We'll be here for a while longer. We'll assist when we can with your partner's security. I'm certain Carbarone's men will make a move sooner or later," Angus added.

"Yeah, I'm positive that Luka and Centron didn't take a liking to being shot in the head by a human female. Those two vampire mixes will want her to suffer when they kill her. So be ready," Quinn said.

"I will be. You'll see. She's worth trying to save."

"Whatever," Angus stated.

Chapter 3

Salina didn't know what she was going to do with herself for the next two weeks. The department put her on limited duty and then the lieutenant placed her on injury leave. Of course Reggie thought it was hysterical and teased her about the lieutenant having a crush on her, but she was annoyed. She suffered a flesh wound. In fact, she was healing exceptionally quickly. She also had this odd sensation inside. It was something she hadn't felt in years. Almost like a separate personality, a creative side that had given her odd dreams as a child and teen. Then one day, they suddenly stopped. It was like she became normal and not some wild crazed freak with crazy dreams about wolves, mystical creatures, and wizards. Maybe as a child she watched the Syfy channel too many times with her dad. But her father seemed to enjoy the shows and movies and got a kick out of the ones about wolves.

She knew that none of those things were real, but in her dreams, as she slept, she remembered hearing people's pleas for help, and somehow she found those in need and assisted. But they had to have been dreams. They felt so real though. She sighed and then stood up and walked across the room.

She looked out the bedroom window at the beautiful sunny day. She should at least try to go for a run, hit the gym, or do something productive. All she needed to do was sit around and eat and be lazy and she would gain twenty pounds.

As she scanned the neighborhood, she thought she noticed someone by the large oak tree on the corner. She looked again, and he was gone. She closed her eyes and shook her head.

What was with the hallucinations lately? From the incident in the old building and seeing the gunman bare his sharp teeth, to seeing Reggie's eyes glow and then the guy in the dark, standing there watching her, too, and now, seeing people hiding in plain sight then disappearing. Had she bumped her head and not remembered? But she did see a few cars that normally weren't parked on her street. Curious, she decided that taking a walk, along with her .22 caliber, might be a great idea. She felt her blood pumping. The need to investigate, her inquisitive mind in overdrive, drove her to leave her town house. She pulled on her sneakers, stuck the gun in the waistband of her shorts, and pulled the tank over it to cover the bulge, and placed her sunglasses on.

Sal started off walking slowly, appearing as if she were merely out for a stroll, remaining within the vicinity of the set of condos on this street. The development was a good size with more than fifty homes. Hers was on the outskirts that bordered some woods that led to a local park and soccer field area.

As she came closer to the vehicles she noticed from her window, she took note that they were empty. It didn't sit right with her gut instincts, and the further she walked, the closer she got to the woods. She felt a mix of emotions. Part of her wanted her to go through the woods and walk to the park. It was a gorgeous, sunny day, and she could use the exercise. But then another part of her felt a forewarning, and her gut instincts kicked in.

She debated about what to do as she came to the beginning of the trail by the woods. She heard something, turned, and nearly screamed at the sight before her. One of the men she shot was standing there, and the son of a bitch was smiling.

* * * *

Quinn and Angus saw the situation begin to unfold right before their eyes. For an investigator, she had screwed up royally. Hadn't she noticed the cars, the man hiding by the woods? Didn't Reggie warn her of the impeding danger to her life? Angus didn't like the feeling he had as Quinn took to the right to head Luka off before he could hurt Sal.

Angus heard her gasp and then pull the gun from under her shirt.

Luka attacked, shifting as he jumped toward her.

The gun went off. Luke roared as they tumbled to the ground. Quinn shifted midair, Sal screamed out in terror, and Quinn connected with Luka, knocking him from Sal.

Angus ran toward her and she pointed the gun and pulled the trigger.

"No, Sal!"

He was furious as he roared and pulled the gun from her hands. His chest burned and he knew he would need to shift in order to heal quickly.

"We are not your enemies."

He inhaled, breathing through his nose rapidly, the anger, the annoyance so strong he could hardly speak when he inhaled her scent. His wolf reacted immediately and he grabbed her, covered her body with his own and sniffed deeply against her neck.

"Get off of me. Who are you? What the hell is that thing? Get off now!" She shoved at him and his cock hardened as he pressed harder against her. He could squash her she was so small compared to him. He tried to speak, to get out everything he needed to say, but he felt confused, aroused, possessive, and protective.

"Don't move." He warned her and then stood up. The pain in his shoulder was getting worse. It was minor considering she had used a .22. But it still burned. Thank God Reggie hadn't given her silver bullets. Behind them Quinn continued to fight when a second shot rang out from a distance. Luka fled and Quinn growled low.

As he made his way closer to them in wolf form, Sal jumped behind Angus.

"What the hell is that? I saw a man and then this beast. Oh God, I'm losing my fucking mind."

"Didn't Reggie explain anything to you?" Angus asked, well, more like growled his question.

"Reggie? You know Reggie?" she asked.

Quinn shifted back, minus clothing, and Sal stared at him, mouth gaped open and hands on her hips.

"What the hell is going on?" she asked, slowly stepping away from both of them.

Quinn inhaled, his nostrils flared, and he started stalking toward Sal. Angus smelt her instant attraction to him. He looked at her and so did Quinn.

She pulled her bottom lip between her teeth and stared at him in shock but also interest.

"Tell me I'm not imagining this. Tell me that you weren't just a big dog only seconds ago. Just tell me and I'll bring myself to the nuthouse."

"Quinn, grab some clothes. Sal, let's get you back to your place." He scrunched his eyes together.

"You're hurt. Who the hell are you and what just happened here?" she asked, stepping toward him and then stepping back.

"Thanks to you and your little peashooter. I'll be fine. Quinn, take her back. I need to shift to heal."

"Angus?"

"Not now, Quinn. Later. When we're alone," he warned his brother. They would talk about what they both smelled and how they must be the crazy ones. Sal couldn't be their mate. Margo was, and she was dead.

* * * *

Sal stared at Quinn. The man was huge, and covered in tattoos. Both men were, but it seemed to her that the one called Angus was in charge. He was talking on his phone, giving orders, and commanding people, definitely not asking them to meet him and Quinn in New York. What was his involvement in this whole situation, and who were the backup he was calling in? The thick Irish brogue proved they weren't from around here, besides them being extra large and very cocky.

She stared at Quinn. He was quiet. He didn't say a word to her, but kept a dead stare at her. Every so often he would inhale and then exhale as if annoyed. He kept flexing his extra large muscles as if they were a reaction to whatever was going on in his head. He had beautiful, full, blond hair. It looked soft. Unlike the thick, hard Irish brogue both he and Angus shared.

Two drop-dead gorgeous men from Ireland who could shift into wolves. What the hell was this world coming to? Why wasn't she running for the exit or calling police for backup? Something held her back. Something deep in her gut, in her heart, made her feel like this was normal and she was safe. She couldn't help but wonder if her dreams were more like premonitions. But she wasn't gifted like that. Give her a crime scene and she could analyze the evidence, come up with a profile, and find the killer or killers. That, she had a gift for.

She thought about her childhood and the memories of her dreams when she was little, but quickly pushed the thoughts away. Those were dreams and they weren't real, just like these men. Something was going on here. Did Reggie have something to do with it? Was this some sort of elaborate joke? It couldn't be. She saw a dead man walking. A man she killed with her own gun, whom every cop and detective who responded to the scene the other day saw dead.

"That guy who tried to attack me. I killed him. I shot him in the head. How the hell could he be alive?" she asked.

"What the fuck were you doing taking a walk by yourself in the fucking woods, lassie?" Quinn asked her. That thick accent of his sure was sexy.

"What the fuck were you doing shifting into a fucking wolf? That's not normal. Who the fuck are you and what type of magic did you use to do that? Is it some sort of mind game? Did you spray me with something when that asshole Luka attacked me?"

He stared at her and appeared as if he clenched his teeth. His eyes suddenly changed from the gray-blue serious ones to a bright yellow with specks of brown. She jumped back and gripped the arms of the couch she sat on.

He showed his incisors. "Does it look like a fucking magic trick?"

She stared at him in awe and trepidation. She shrugged her shoulders.

If she weren't so freaked out right now, she would actually analyze the sensations that these two men were causing in her body. Both Angus and Quinn made her breasts feel full, her nipples hard, and her pussy actually ache. They were so freaking attractive. She never met men as big, as sexy, and as muscular as these men. They were a living, walking fantasy and she was feeling pretty damn ready to hit on them. Which was completely odd. She closed her eyes and took a deep breath as she willed her tough attitude to resurface and not make her so vulnerable to their sex appeal.

She was experiencing flashes in her mind of them having sex. It had to be due to her lack of any sexual encounters for the past couple of years. She never met any man she felt compelled to have sex with. Not since college and even that was more of a show of independence and control over her life and her body. Not that she had regrets. Keano was a hottie and a half. In fact, if he lived locally, she wouldn't hesitate calling him for a little friends-with-benefits action. She swallowed hard. These two men were not anything like men around here. Her attraction was instant, and that in itself freaked her out a little.

She swallowed hard then glanced at Angus, who disconnected the call, then glanced back toward Quinn. He was smirking as if he knew what his good looks and sensational body were doing to her.

He inhaled and stared at her breasts. Could he smell her arousal? *Jerk.*

Just then the front door shoved open and neither Quinn or Angus turned to look. Angus said hello to Reggie as if he knew it were him.

"Sal. Holy shit, are you okay?" he asked, hurrying toward her and kneeling on the floor in front of her. The moment he covered her hands with his and was close to her, Quinn growled low. Reggie looked toward him, eyes wide, and Sal pulled Reggie next to her, closer. Quinn growled deeper.

"Reggie, don't mess with him. He isn't normal," she whispered.

"Normal?" Reggie asked and then looked at Angus and Quinn.

"Luka attacked. Quinn needed to shift, then I did because she shot me," Angus stated, his brogue sounding even stronger. Maybe that was because he was still pissed off at her? He rubbed his hand along his chest where the bullet had been. She was still recovering from the fact that she shot him and he was fine. He didn't need medical attention, he just complained that the area itched. Then again, Luka was alive and well, and she shot him with her Glock right in the forehead. How the fuck did someone survive that?

"Shit. Okay. Sal, there are some things we need to go over," Reggie began to say.

"I can't believe that you didn't warn her. What the fuck were you thinking? That this asshole and his goons would go away? She shot his two main guys, his son. Of course Carbarone would come for her as revenge," Angus reprimanded Reggie.

"Revenge? Son? What is he talking about, Reggie?" she asked.

He covered her knees with his hands. Quinn growled low.

"Easy, brother. He is our cousin after all."

"What in God's name are you talking about? You guys are cousins?"

"Sal, listen to me. We'll deal with the rest later, for now you need to know a few things." He started to explain about the existence of werewolves, of other mystical creatures, and the fact that the two men she shot in the head and thought she killed were actually half wolves, half vampires. He went on and on with Quinn and Angus watching over them and Angus's phone going off continuously. He obviously was very important. A few times he held a finger to his temple and stared off as if he were thinking hard. She wondered what that was about.

"Okay, I'm totally freaked out here and lost. Let me bypass the craziness that there are men and women that can shift into wolves, and other mystical creatures. I can't believe I just said that. God, okay, let me try to understand here, for argument's sake. Why would they care about coming after me if they have such special abilities? I'm just a human. How could it be fun to mess with me and kill me when I don't offer a challenge?" she asked Reggie.

"You do now. Luka failed. This will gain Carbarone's interest."

"He'll definitely want her now. He'll find out she's special, then he'll do to her what he did to Margo," Quinn stated and Angus now looked about ready to hit something.

"Special?" she asked.

"Sal, just bear with us for a bit. There's a lot to explain."

"Obviously, and to tell you the truth, you lost me during the entire 'ability to shift and vampires existing' part. Just tell me how to defend myself against these things. Do I need a special magic potion, some special bullets, or do I have to stab them in the heart with a wooden stake? Or is steel better so it doesn't break?"

She couldn't believe this, but maybe watching all those Syfy movies would pay off.

"Sal!" Reggie yelled her name and she stopped talking and started at his angry expression.

"This is not the fucking movies. This is the real deal. Forget about all the bullshit you heard about or read about in books or saw in the movies. Just focus on what I tell you and what Angus and Quinn tell you. We're going to have to leave here. You need constant protection and I can't provide it for you accordingly while also investigating Carbarone," Reggie told her.

"I don't need bodyguards. I'm perfectly capable of taking care of myself. Just give me the tools to counter their attacks. I'll handle the rest."

Quinn chuckled.

"What? You think I can't?" She challenged him and his smirk changed to an angry expression as he looked her body over.

"A tiny thing like you needs men like us and our abilities to protect you."

She stood up. "You know, at first I was kind of liking you, and thinking for a pretty big guy you're agile and attractive, but now I see the real you."

"The real me?"

"Yeah, a chauvinistic asshole who thinks all women are weak and incapable of being warriors."

He eyed her over and she hated her damn body's reaction.

"You talk tough but you can't handle these monsters. They'll eat you alive."

"Should I be worried about you, too, considering you're like one of those monsters?"

He eyed her over and Angus spoke up. "Cool it. We're not the bad guys. We're going to protect you from these men."

She walked across the room, arms crossed, and mind going in a thousand directions. "And if I don't want your help?"

"Then you die," Angus stated firmly, his gray-blue eyes holding hers intently.

She looked toward Reggie.

"They're my cousins. We will need their protection. Look at what could have happened today," he added.

She was going to say more but then her own cell phone started ringing. She looked at the caller ID and saw that it was her father.

"Hi, Dad."

He immediately carried on about what happened and about trusting the Fennigan brothers. He also asked that she come to his house tonight to go over some things.

"I'll be there," she whispered as Angus and Quinn stared at her.

* * * *

Angus was in shock. He couldn't understand how this happened. How could Sal be their mate when Margo was? He was certain that a chance like this was rare. To find another mate when their first one had been taken and murdered. He couldn't help but wonder if Sal was meant for his other brothers as well. They'd find out soon enough. They were headed to them now.

Angus was filled with a lot of emotions. Being an Alpha wolf and leader, he didn't analyze his emotions. In fact, when Margo was murdered, taken from him and his brothers, his heart had shattered. They hadn't even gotten the opportunity to pursue their mate and consummate the relationship. It happened so quickly. One day Margo was there and the next she was gone.

He felt the anger, the need for revenge fill what was left of his heart. He watched Sal, uncertain if he even had it in him to be her mate. Perhaps he would leave it up to his brothers. After all, he failed one mate. Maybe he would fail Sal, too.

But her scent, her beauty was so enticing. He had difficulty admitting to himself that this connection felt deep, and instantly strong. As much as he wanted to claim her, he feared doing so for the simple fact that she could die and be taken from him just as Margo was.

"She'll need us to attend a dinner with her father tonight," Reggie stated.

"We have to meet up with Van Fagan and Vanderlan, too," Angus replied.

"You meet up with them while Reggie and I head to Sal's father's," Quinn said.

Angus thought about that a moment. Truth was, as much as he didn't want to leave her side, he knew Quinn could handle her protection. Angus needed to discuss things with Van and Vanderlan so they could make a plan to destroy Carbarone together.

Chapter 4

"Just lie still, my dear. This is only going to hurt a little bit," Vargon Carbarone whispered as he straddled the female's body. She was a wolf with Skylar pack, and someone of importance to their bloodline. If he could force a mating upon her and get her to side with him, then he would have another in to the pack and taking it over. He needed to expand and if he had to birth a shitload of cubs then he would.

"I don't think that the spell is quite strong enough. I need something more. She's going to die just like the others." Torque, the wizard, told Vargon Carbarone.

"Please don't hurt me. Please, I have children and a mate," she whispered, sounding so weak and fragile. Vargon had bitten her multiple times. It was all she kept saying over and over again. She had a mate. She had children. Who gave a shit? If this didn't work, then she was dead and he would get another to replace her.

Torque chanted some sort of phrase with his eyes closed and his hands palms forward toward Vargon and the woman. She was quite lovely. Long brown hair, big brown eyes, and a fairly decent body. Easy prey. But it seemed she was lacking something, too.

"It's not working. Her bloodline is not strong enough to force the mating past her other mate's binding."

The gurgling sound filled the room. Vargon sat up and stared at the dying woman as she took her last breath.

He climbed off her body and then pulled on the robe. "Get her out of my sight." He looked at Torque. "You need to figure out a way to make this work. I must have something that can help me take possession of Skylar Pack."

"You may be forced to do this the old-fashioned way, by challenging the Alpha."

"Ha! Like I would do that."

"You could have one of your sons or even nephews do it. They are loyal to you, and they can stand in position of Alpha, challenge McCarthy, and kill him. Then they can relinquish control to you behind the scenes."

Vargon stared at the lifeless body on the bed and thought about Torque's words.

"We'll give it a little more time. Let's get the money in order, continue to rip off the unknowing Were packs so I have financial backing before I strike. Then maybe one of my Alphas can challenge Skylar Pack. I'll have to wait and see."

* * * *

"Thank goodness you're okay," Pierce Santos stated as Sal hugged her father.

"I'm fine, Daddy. In fact I feel a hundred percent already and can't wait to get back to work. I think Reggie is going to call Lieutenant McCallister for me and get things moving faster." She eyed Reggie, who crossed his arms in front of his chest and shook his head.

"The lieutenant wants you safe and fully recovered. He cares a lot about your daughter, too, Pierce," Reggie said as he walked over and shook Pierce's hand. Sal gave Reggie a light punch in his shoulder.

She walked over toward the living room and sat down on the couch.

"Pierce, meet Quinn Fennigan, my cousin."

Her father shook Quinn's hand and seemed impressed with Quinn's size and height. She was pretty impressed, too. The man was very big. But she had to remind herself that he turned into a huge, vicious dog in the snap of a finger. That was not something she was swallowing too well.

"I recall Reggie speaking of you and your brothers. You reside in Ireland, don't you?" he asked.

"Well, the brogue kind of gives that away," Reggie said and then plopped down onto the couch next to Sal.

Quinn gave Reggie a dirty look and then sat in the recliner.

She had a feeling Quinn wanted to sit next to her, too.

She wasn't sure how she felt about that. He and his brother were intimidating to say the least, but their brogues were so sexy. Every time they spoke, she stared and listened intently.

"We're all over the world, working wherever we're needed," Quinn told her father.

"All over the world? I thought you were part of some police force in Ireland," Sal asked.

He turned to look at her. His eyes roamed over her body. It seemed habitual for him and it made her feel both attractive and on the defensive. It was as if he gave her his full, undivided attention. What man did that when talking to a woman?

"My brothers and I are part of a task force. We assist in various aspects of criminal justice."

"Well, are you part of the investigation to help take down these men who are now after my daughter?" Pierce asked.

Reggie leaned forward.

"Pierce, we're trying to bring your daughter up to speed about what we're dealing with."

"Up to speed?"

"Yes, we started explaining about the supernatural beings that walk this earth and live among the humans. She saw with her own eyes the reality of werewolves shifting, thanks to Quinn here." Reggie gave him a wink and Quinn glared at his cousin.

Pierce leaned forward. "Have you spoken about her mother?"

"No. No there's no need to get into that right now. I think it's better that we stick to keeping her safe and surrounded by her mates," Reggie stated.

"Mates?" Pierce asked, raising his voice.

"My mother? What would Mom have to do with this? She's been dead for years. And what's with the mate crap?" Sal asked, feeling her insides tingle at the use of the word mate. Especially with Quinn in the room.

"She'll need to know. It may be time, Reggie," Pierce told them.

"Time for what?" Quinn asked.

At least he looked just as perplexed as Sal felt.

"Yeah, time for what?" Sal asked.

Reggie ran his fingers through his hair.

"First off, Pierce, Quinn and Angus are Sal's mates."

"What?" Pierce asked.

"How can that be? What about Margo, the healer?" Pierce asked.

"Who is Margo?" Sal questioned.

Quinn looked angry. "Angus and I are just as confused. You know about our other mate?"

"Wait a minute. Hold on one second. Can we backstep a little here? What is a mate? What happened to their other mate, Margo, you said her name was."

"Sal, wolves mate to secure their bloodline, to procreate, and to bind families' bloodlines for generations. When a wolf finds their mate and bonds, they bond for life. It's a lot like marriage," Reggie explained.

"Hold on one second. First, I am not a wolf. I'm human. Second, I can't be part of something like that. I don't even date. I'm a workaholic. I live for locking up shithead criminals and fighting on the streets against the bad guys. I can't be a mate to anyone."

It was odd, but even as she said the words, she felt this strange sensation inside and she looked at Quinn. He held her gaze and his eyes slightly glowed. She swallowed hard.

"It is true, Sal. Angus and I, and perhaps our other brothers, are your mates. We'll know soon enough when they arrive."

She shook her head. "How can one woman be the mate to more than one man? You don't mean like—"

She gasped as she realized it meant mating sexually, binding them all together. A woman mated to multiple men meant she would be a sex slave, stuck in bed for the rest of her life probably bearing children for them to expand their wolf packs.

She stood up with fists by her side and glared at Quinn.

"I'm not your mate. I don't have sex with multiple men at once. I will not be a baby machine so you can expand your packs or whatever. I'm a human female with rights. Besides, what happened to your last mate? You and your brothers get bored with her and tossed her out?" She raised her voice.

"Sal!" Both Reggie and Pierce reprimanded her.

She felt the ache to her heart the moment the words left her lips. She sensed something, yet her mind was clouded by odd images. She was definitely headed toward the loony bin.

"She was murdered, taken from us before we could mate and bond. Not all wolves find their mates. When they do, it's powerful and they instantly become possessive and protective. But we hadn't protected her. We allowed her out of our sight because she was a healer. She was helping the Goddesses of the Circle, who are the legal authority on all Were law and supernatural law, when she was killed."

"Sal, it's rare, practically unheard of, for wolves to get a second chance and find another mate. But the gods and goddesses have spoken. They've brought you together with your men and you must embrace it. You need their protection."

She looked at Reggie and then her father. She paced the room, and could feel all their eyes upon her but especially Quinn's. It was surreal how she felt his stare more deeply than the others. Or was she imagining it? She could in fact be losing her mind.

Then she thought about the situation today near her home. Quinn and Angus were there. Were they watching over her or was it the man who attacked her? Why were they there unless it was the men they wanted. Quinn and Angus came here from Ireland. Fucking Ireland. Something didn't add up. Then it hit her.

"The man who came after me, was he the one responsible for killing your mate?" she asked Quinn.

He appeared as if he were biting the inside of his cheek.

"Vargon Carbarone, Luka's father, had a hand in her death."

"So this is why these men are after me? They know that I'm your mate, they killed your last one, and so they want to kill me now?" she asked.

"They don't know that we are mates. But they will find out," Quinn stated.

"Honey, they want to kill you because you put bullets to their heads. You need Quinn and Angus's protection," Reggie said.

She stared at Quinn. "Seems to me these guys want to kill me, whatever they are, because you and Angus say I'm your mate. You're the ones who put me in danger and now you feel obligated to protect me."

Quinn stood up, towering over her. She wouldn't take a retreating step back. The man was definitely used to giving orders and being respected. He had to be six feet four inches tall, and muscles on top of muscles. She swallowed hard.

"You don't know these men, these monsters, or what they're capable of. My brothers and I do, and being that you are our mate we're going to do everything in our power to protect you. That includes keeping you by our side and teaching you what your position as our mate exactly is."

"I am not your mate or whatever. I will not be 'taught' how to open my thighs, bare children, and take orders from a bunch of barbaric men I don't even know." She turned away from him.

She heard a low growl and before she could turn toward Quinn, her father grabbed her arm and pulled her along with him.

"Let me talk to her, Quinn. Explain a few things," Pierce said. She glanced at Quinn, who looked ready to tear her apart. So much for caring for his mate and protecting her. It seemed he wanted to do her harm.

* * * *

"You have always been strong willed. Despite the spell that the fairies placed on you as a child, your true personality has shown through." Her father walked with her to the family library. He led her to the couch and she immediately took a seat and stared at him with that inquisitive expression he adored about his daughter.

He pulled the picture frame of her mother down from the mantle.

He thought about his beautiful wife, Athlena, and about the day they met.

"Your mother was the most beautiful woman I had ever laid eyes on. She captured my heart immediately." He handed her the picture. Salina gently ran her finger along the picture.

"I wish I had gotten more time with her. I only remember little things about her. The smell of her perfume, light, floral, and the softness of her skin against my cheek when she hugged me," Salina said.

"She adored you. She, too, had a special gift, just as you do."

Her eyes scrunched together as she looked at him inquisitively. "Gift?"

"Yes, Salina. Without wasting too much time or getting too deeply into it, your mother was a Magi, a woman of mystical, magic abilities. She could speak to every type of creature and knew every language of all living things. She could see things, sense things about people. Being so powerful, she was sought after by many types of mystical creatures. Her parents had to place a spell on her, too, in order to ensure she wasn't taken by someone of evil mind and soul. We actually met, fell in love, and realized that we were mates."

"Are you a Magi, as you called it, too?" she asked, pulling her bottom lip between her teeth.

"No. My bloodline consists of wizards and warlocks. Unfortunately I was one of the weaker ones. Or so I thought until I met your mother. As mates we joined, and when that happened, her protective field was raised, and her identity revealed. I wasn't with her when they attacked, when these men, these monsters working for some rogue Alpha wolf attacked and took her from me. Somehow she called for help in protecting you and a spell was placed over you as well."

"What happened to her? They killed her?"

"They took her away. He tried to force her to mate with him and to protect his packs and build his empire so he could take over as ruler. She sacrificed her life for yours. She was killed once she ensured that you were safe and not identified as a Magi."

"Oh God, that's terrible. You were working in the police department then. You had that accident."

"There wasn't an accident, Salina. I was trying to fight off the rogue wolves who were taking my mate from me. There was one individual who wanted your mother for himself. He is the one I tried to battle, but he had an army. I wasn't strong enough. I failed her, and would have failed you if not for your mother's love and power of magic to protect you."

"Oh God, this is crazy. Yet, it's like I've known something was different about me for so long. I've had these dreams, these visions," she said as she stood up and walked slowly around the room. He could tell that she was at least taking the information seriously. His daughter had always been a critic, saw the glass as half-empty, and trust was not easily earned in her eyes. That determination, that fight to be on top, led her to her position in the police department. She was an amazing detective and she loved her job. But now that her mates had found her, her destiny might lay elsewhere.

"I don't know all you're capable of, what your mother may or may not have passed down to you. All I know is that once your identity is revealed, you're no longer safe but at risk."

"You mean by the men, the wolves who took Mom?"

"By any Alpha supernatural out there who wants to use your power for evil. The one who took your mom is dead as far as I know. I wanted to seek revenge, but I had you to watch over and protect since you were such a gift, a powerful weapon of the Magi and of the world. Your position in law enforcement is commendable and it has great meaning. You're a protector. You are an investigator who seeks justice for victims and their families. It's all part of who you are. But now that your identity is at risk of being revealed, and if in fact the shield the fairies placed over you for protection begins to weaken so your mates can seal the bond between you, then you are in grave danger just like your mother. We didn't know, Salina. If we had, if I had understood her power and position, then I would have never left her side, even for a moment. That's why it's important to accept the protection of your intended mates. Without them you're susceptible to being taken and forced to conduct evil, or worse, you'll die."

"But you don't even know if I have these powers. You don't know what they are or could be. I may not be of any importance at all. How will I know? When will these powers be revealed to me? What am I supposed to do now?"

"You need to accept the guidance and protection of the Fennigan men. As Alphas to the royal family, to the Circle, to Princess Ava, the Irish Jewel, these men are very strong and powerful. It leads me to believe that the evil that will come after you is great. You will need the power of such strong, superior wolves."

"No, no, I can't accept this. You're throwing all this information at me and I'm just supposed to process it and accept it? I can't do that. I'm an investigator, I'm inquisitive, I push for answers, for an understanding of everything. I can't just accept this because you say it's so. This huge-ass wolf man comes here and states he's my mate along with his god knows how many brothers. No."

"Sal, it is your destiny. The magic that has hidden your abilities, your true identity, will be lifted. Not all at once, but as you grow stronger, believe deeper in what you really are, and accept it as your fate, the magic will come full force. Then, it will all become clear who you are, what your position is, and what you are responsible for. You are special, as I have always known. You need to listen to your senses, your gut instincts. You're more than capable of that. You do it on a daily basis. It's what has helped you to be such a successful investigator. The Fennigan Pack are great warriors. The gods and goddesses do not make mistakes. The sooner you accept your fate, the easier and safer life will be. You are special in so many ways."

"Special how? What is the power I have? What am I supposed to do with it? Can it help me to stop people from killing? Can it help me bring justice to families who have lost loved ones to murder? What?"

"Salina, you possess two very special gifts. The gift of the Magi, the one who can see, help heal all those living things that walk this realm and all others. But, you also contain my family's genes. It bypassed over me, giving me half the power and strength of my father and other rulers. You could very well be a very powerful wizard. Only time can tell, but either of these powers in the wrong hands could mean big trouble for all mystical creatures, including your mates. You can see how the bad guys, these rogue wolves would love to possess you. If they were to gain control of you and your abilities, it could mean a hell of a fight to defend Were and mystical law throughout all realms. Usually Magis and wizards do not mate. In doing so there are some aspects of our abilities that can be persuaded, corrupted, and overtaken. It's complicated to explain, and most don't know this, but certain people do. It's better to keep you hidden than to expose you to the dangers of being taken and used for evil purposes."

"But I don't feel anything. I don't feel like a Magi or a wizard or as if I have power. I've always obeyed the laws. Hell, I uphold the laws. How could I be susceptible to breaking the laws? I don't feel anything. In fact right now I feel like I'm losing my mind and all of this is make-believe. Why can't I feel the powers and identify them?"

"That is because of the spell placed on you by a very powerful and loving fairy, Bethany. It seems they're aware of your power and abilities, and as precaution they placed the spell on you to protect you from harm. This is not make-believe. This is all real. Trust me, sweetheart, as you accept your fate with your mates, you will become stronger, identify your abilities, and one day it will all be revealed to you."

"Do these men know about my abilities and what I am?"

"They can only sense that you are their mate. But as you begin to accept them, the wall, the shield will thin, revealing not only your Magi and possibly wizard powers, but also revealing how powerful you are. If you deny the connection, the bond with your mates, you not only put yourself at risk, but also your mates and all the people and mystical creatures you are meant to protect and serve. Please, Salina. You must keep an open mind. Trust me that I am not lying or misguiding you. Most importantly, trust your mates, for they will give their lives for you just as I would."

"This is a lot to take in. I don't know what to think."

"It will be revealed to you in time."

"But why is the spell still on me? I'm twenty-five years old. I think I have a pretty damn good head on my shoulders, so why still maintain the spell?"

"It has to do with your training, abilities, and simply right timing when you find and identify your intended mates. Although I get the feeling that your time is coming. Mating can secure your safety and position. The Fennigan Pack consists of six very intelligent, strong, powerful, Alpha Weres who will protect you and guide you through the training and learning you'll need. It's another reassurance, protective shield for the Circle and the goddesses. If you were to be taken, controlled by evil rogues like Carbarone, or the one who attempted to take your mother, it could mean destruction of security around the Goddess of the Circle, the Circle of Elders, and all other secret organizations that exist around the universe."

"Holy shit. Who was the one who took Mommy?" she asked.

Her father lowered his head and took a deep breath. "That's not important right now. He is gone. Disappeared from this realm. What's important is that you follow your heart and your gut even if the decisions are terrifying. That instinct is there despite the spell of protection. It will be your greatest weapon."

"I can't believe this, yet I'm not totally freaked out about it either. It's like I know it but it's not fully processing in my mind, only in my heart and gut deep within me. Holy crap." She leaned back on the couch.

"But why would I help them? The bad guys that is?"

"They, too, have people who possess manipulating power and mind control. If you're exposed, and not strong enough mentally, confident and loyal at a hundred percent, then it could happen and they could take over. That is why it's so crucial for you to be mated, to accept your fate as the goddesses have proclaimed."

"No. No, not me. I wouldn't go to the dark side, Dad. But I wish I could understand what exactly it means, having all these powers. Like what exactly? Why do I need mates to assist me? Why can't I do this alone? I've done everything on my own. I don't ask for help. I don't allow men especially to do things for me. So why now?"

"The gods have spoken, Salina. They will guide you. The gifts you possess will come to you. The individuals you can trust your heart, your powers will allow you to see and you will know. You'll feel it in your heart. I can sense the walls of the spell thinning. That could mean that the fairies are letting you learn about your powers through them or that it's getting closer to destroying the cover you have. If that's the case, then please, Salina, you must stay with the Fennigan men and mate with them. They are your destiny."

"These gods you talk about, you trust, how can you when they took the woman you loved away? They caused her death. You expect me to follow a god, gods, goddesses, or whatever, who do such things? Who allowed my mother to be vulnerable to an attack? They're to blame, not you, for not knowing how susceptible my mother would be once you mated. No, Father, I'm not making the same mistake. I don't want to engage in any mating ritual. I'll fight this battle whatever may come. I'll accept my fate, but I'll have a hand in the direction it's going in, not anyone or anything else."

* * * *

Vanderlan looked at Angus, feeling his own shock at the situation.

"So you have another mate? How is that possible?" Van asked Angus.

Angus was sitting in a chair, head down, appearing completely shocked.

"I have no fucking idea. I was hoping that Dani could give me some insight into this."

"I'm sure she can. She's going to have a lot of different emotions about this as well. Her and Margo were best friends. Margo taught her everything about being a healer," Van added.

Angus looked up. "I don't think I can accept this. I don't think I have it in me," he said, his Irish brogue thick with emotion.

Vanderlan placed his hand on his shoulder. "Angus, the gods and goddesses do things for reasons we may not understand, but usually good comes of those decisions. You can't fight the mating bond."

"Says who?" Angus asked, standing up and pacing the room.

"Angus, think about the current situation. Carbarone and his pack are responsible for Margo's death. He is working on something.

Obviously the gods and goddesses want you and your brothers to be aware of it. You can't leave Sal unprotected."

"I'll leave it to Quinn and my brothers if they are her mates as well."

"That is not going to work and you know it," Vanderlan added.

"Enough talk about it. I'll deal with it on my own. Now, looking into Carbarone's business transactions, did you come up with anything suspicious?" he asked them.

Vanderlan could hear Dani's thoughts in his head. He had projected the conversation to her, heard her gasps, felt her emotions as tears streamed down her cheeks. He wished he was with her right now to console her, but then he felt Randolph and Benjamin holding her. Baher and Miele joined her next.

Tell Angus that this is meant to be. Tell him that Margo would want him and his brothers to be happy and be together. I have a feeling that there will be more danger ahead for Angus and his brothers, but especially for Sal. She is of great importance to the Were community and existence. Tell him, Vanderlan.

Vanderlan heard Dani's words just as Van had.

"Angus, Dani speaks to us now. She is just as shocked and emotional for you, yet she says that there is danger ahead and that Sal is special to the Were community," Van told him.

"Special? How? She's human."

"I don't know and neither does Dani, but trust that the gods and goddesses do things for a reason. You need to protect Sal," Vanderlan added.

"Well, I'll think about it. So what do you have on Carbarone? Anything thus far?" Angus asked, still being stubborn and keeping a shield over his emotions. Vanderlan knew he was suffering and he hoped that Angus didn't push Sal away to protect himself from his own fears and emotions.

"Well, you and Quinn were right about Carbarone being up to some illegal activities. We have teams in place watching him, and the avenue of illegal drugs and prostitution. But that's not the half of it. He's been giving a lot of money to a corporation in Ireland. Not sure what they produce, or if it's pharmaceuticals to enhance his drug business. We asked Willie and Declan Pack to look into it. Ava has pretty good control over operations across Ireland and keeping things legit. But shit still happens. There's always rogue wolves being greedy and trying to establish their own pack power. Perhaps Carbarone is doing the same," Van said.

"Do you think he's trying to grow his pack in a takeover attempt?" Angus asked.

Vanderlan felt his own concern grow. "The only pack small enough to be taken over would be Skylar Pack. They have locations scattered throughout the world, including Ireland and right here in New York," Vanderlan told them.

"Well, then a visit to their Alpha, McCarthy, may be necessary," Van stated.

"I'll take care of it. If this is the case. If Carbarone is planning a takeover to gain more power, then we need to stop him. Perhaps gathering enough evidence against him will finally get the Circle of Elders to rule him rogue and sentence him for all his crimes," Angus said then pulled out his cell to make a call, an inquiry about a possible takeover.

Chapter 5

"Who is this woman, that she's able to escape you twice in a forty-eight-hour period?" Vargon Carbarone asked his son, Luka, as he stood in the home office. Their penthouse in Manhattan was top notch. Carbarone barely stayed here. His permanent resident in mountains and woods of Nevada was where he enjoyed staying for a better part of the year. But business was booming, and despite all the changes amongst the Circle of Elders and their new appointees, he had money to make and smaller packs to squash.

"She had help."

"Help?" he asked Luka. His son didn't reply immediately. "Well. Who?"

"Quinn and Angus Fennigan."

Carbarone swung his head around to look at his son. He wasn't completely shocked, although he heard the Fennigan men were now weak and still mourning their mate, Margo. She had to die. It was how he saved the wizard Torque from being exiled to another realm. Carbarone had pulled a fast one on Margo, getting her to assist a needy, injured Were who was caught in the line of fire as a demon attempted to kill the goddesses.

He smiled. Torque proved to be quite resourceful and loyal immediately. Now he was helping Carbarone to gain some extra power so he could take over Skylar Pack territories. But he was feeling a bit discouraged. He had forced himself on three different female wolves from Skylar Pack who were high in the bloodline but the bond didn't take. In fact, the women died even with the assistance of Torque and his wizard powers. He needed to find another woman. He needed power.

"So, the Fennigan men know this woman? Who is she and what is their relationship?" he asked.

"I don't know. They were protecting her, and they are cousins with Reggie. But it was only Quinn and Angus there. The others weren't."

Carbarone rubbed his chin. "I wonder why. And where is this woman now? Who did you say she was?"

"She's just a human. A partner in the police department with Reggie. She doesn't give off a scent of any kind. Hardly could tell she was only human and nothing more. I'm pretty certain that she's harmless. Perhaps they helped her because Reggie is their cousin?"

"Well then, why can't you kill her?"

"I tried."

"Interesting. Well, I have more important things for you to work on right now. I'm trying to seal the deal with Torque in taking over Skylar Pack territory. We have our men in position, and Torque is going to assist us."

"Well, then why do you need me?" Luka asked.

"I need you to assist him and tag along as Alpha. Bring your crew with you."

"But what about the woman, Sal?"

"What about her? She's a measly human. We have important Were business to conduct. With my hand in the security business now, we can definitely infiltrate some of the higher-ups personal finances. Torque can ensure that nothing is traceable and we will be filthy rich off the hard work of others. It's the perfect plan."

"But the woman," Luka said again.

Carbarone raised his voice. "What about her?"

"She's beautiful and tough. I wanted you to see her."

"She is lovely enough that you would bring her to me alive?"

"Yes, Father. There is something about her I think you will enjoy. But mostly, she gained the interest of those two fucking wolves, Quinn and Angus. I hate them. I want them dead."

"Hmm. As do I, but they are too well connected by blood to the Fagan Pack, Declan, Dolberg, and the damn Goddess of the Circle herself. But I understand your interest. It would be pleasurable to grab a hold of something else they like and take it out of their grasp. Leave them alone for now. Upon our return you can play your little game."

"But, Father, what if Angus and Quinn get to enjoy her first, before me? Then what?"

He tapped a finger against his chin. "Let me put your cousin Jaydin on it. He'll be sure to get the correct information on her. In fact he can get her to me if need be. That wolf doesn't back down to anyone."

Luka nodded his head.

"Prepare to leave within the hour."

"Yes, Father." Luka left the room and Carbarone glanced at the files on his desk. "This is going to be so simple, and Torque is going to love seeking his revenge on the royal families."

* * * *

Sal's head was pounding. Talk about information overload. She felt about ready to lose it. Reggie, her dad, and Quinn explained a lot to her in a small amount of time. The things standing out in her head right now with Quinn driving his SUV and her attraction growing stronger were the facts about bonding, getting bitten, uniting with wolves, and mating for life. She was grateful that her father and Reggie hadn't mentioned her mother, her potential magic abilities, or anything she discussed with her dad. Then these wolves would latch on and not let her go. She couldn't even imagine getting intimately involved with such ginormous men. They weren't even human. Plus there were six of them. What if their brothers were part of this, too, and the gods supposedly bound her to them? Then what?

She wasn't a virgin, so no worries there. In fact, she considered herself pretty self-sufficient and definitely not in need of a man, or anyone for that matter, to take care of her. But she also knew that men were intimidated, maybe even turned off, by a woman who was overly independent. She knew how to tone it down, just as she knew how to turn it up when the guys came sniffing for some easy lay.

It took a lot for her to spread her legs for a man. Her sexual encounters though few, were hot and satisfying, but not even the attraction she felt to those men she had sex with affected her quite like the pull she felt around Quinn and Angus. It was hard to describe, but she was more than attracted to them. She was beginning to lust for them.

She licked her lips and tried to ignore the burning in her core. Her pussy felt like tiny spasms of awareness stimulated it deep below her skin. She closed her eyes and instantly saw Quinn and Angus. They were so fucking huge, though. How the hell would they not hurt her when they made love to her?

She shook her head. It wasn't going to be love. It was like some sort of contractual agreement amongst the gods and goddesses who supposedly ran the universe. What they said, what they predicted or caused, was meant to be and there was no defying it.

She felt a bit frustrated but then came those feelings again. She looked out the window. They would be back to her place shortly. It was late and she wondered if Reggie would stay, or would he leave her alone with Quinn? Was Angus back already, too? Would she be alone with two monstrosities of sexual eye candy?

She released a sigh. *Okay, worst scenario. I let them fuck me. I have sex with them and maybe it's more than just satisfying. Their cocks could be as big as the rest of them.* She swallowed hard, making a sound with her throat. Her face felt flush. *Then what happens? They start making demands, telling me what to do, stop me from working? Shit. No fucking way.*

"I'm not going to quit my job. I love being a detective and I love law enforcement and locking up criminals. You, and no one else, five brothers or more, aren't going to change that," she blurted out as Quinn parked the SUV.

Quinn glanced at her, but gave no verbal response, so Reggie spoke.

"Well, I'm going to head home. Quinn will be staying with you, and Angus is probably upstairs already or on the way. I know this was a lot to take in, Sal, but try to stay open minded, and listen to Quinn. He can help you with any questions or concerns you might have."

She got out of the car, huffing and annoyed, yet nervous and a bit stimulated. She was going to be alone with Quinn and maybe even Angus. Was something going to happen tonight?

Reggie gave her a hug and then headed toward his car. Quinn held his keys in his hand and stared at her.

"Ready?"

She rolled her eyes and headed inside.

"We'll talk about your job and the changes in all our lives once my brothers get here."

"Wonderful. So it will be six against one."

He grabbed her upper arm as they stepped by her front door. Quinn reached down and placed his hand against her cheek. She was frozen in place.

Quinn, just like Angus, wore his sex appeal like cologne. It seemed to waft through the air and attack all her senses, turning her mind to mush. Her breasts felt full, and her pussy leaked. Hell, he was fucking hot, who was she kidding.

"All I ask of you right now is to follow your gut. Listen to your body, and let yourself feel what's right there."

She stared up at his lips, her head tilted far back, making her neck ache. He had strong, firm lips, and the sound of the last syllable of his sentence, brogue and all, tingled through her center. She needed to get a grip and maintain her control here. There was a lot to think about and digest. She didn't need to rush into this. Her mom wasn't a homicide detective on the city streets of New York. Sal was well trained and gung ho. She could handle most situations and she'd handle this, too.

"I don't know you. I don't even know if I trust you."

He brushed his thumb along her lower lip. She could feel his extra large, warm hand against her hip bone, and the significant difference in size heightened her arousal.

"You'll learn to trust my brothers and I, lassie. You'll see."

She thought he might kiss her, but then he paused and appeared as if he were thinking something right before he opened her front door without the key.

She felt disappointed, which shocked her, and then she noticed Angus.

Sal took a deep breath. The sight of the man, extra large in his upper body, with a hard expression and a determined look in his gray-blue eyes, made her pussy clench. Both men inhaled then growled low as Quinn closed the door.

Suddenly embarrassed that perhaps what Reggie and her father told her was true, that wolves had impeccable senses of smell and could even distinguish wolf packs just from sniffing someone, she tried to escape being this close to them.

"Well, I'm going to call it a night. I understand that you'll both be sticking around, so help yourself to whatever. There are sheets and pillows in the hallway closet. That sofa turns into a pullout bed and there's another bedroom down the hall," she said, motioning with her arm around her small home.

Angus looked her over as she hurried toward her room. Could she chance a shower and new clothes with them here, or would they break down the door and take her then, in the shower? She tightened up and then felt the leak of moisture. *Goddamn it, I'm losing my mind. I just need to go to bed. Yes, bed will help me forget about everything. I'm so damn tired.*

* * * *

"So she seems accepting then to all the information you explained?" Angus asked as Quinn and his brother heard the shower go on in the bathroom. He couldn't help but to think about what her body may look like. He could tell Sal had a great ass and big breasts. But she was muscular, toned, not petite or fragile, which would be a good thing considering how huge he and his brothers were. He still couldn't believe that she was their mate. Or at least his and Quinn's. He hoped she belonged to the others. It could bring them back together and help them reunite their brotherhood. That thought brought on a surge of inadequacy he had been fighting since Margo's murder. He'd failed her, and he could fail Sal. Giving his brothers full possession of her seemed like the best option.

"She seemed okay, and was thinking about things on the way back over here. She blurted out something about keeping her job and that she wouldn't quit because we would make demands. Oh, and forget those crazy thoughts you're trying to block me from hearing. You're not leaving us. You're part of this and we'll need you." Quinn lifted his feet up and placed them on the coffee table. He leaned back against the sofa.

"I have not made my final decision. But whatever it may be, your job will be to ensure Sal's safety. I give full power and leadership of that to you."

"What the hell are you talking about? You're the Alpha. It's your place to mate with her first, to bite her and seal the deal. Myself and the others follow. Nothing has changed the rules and the process."

"Margo's death changed it," Angus snapped at Quinn.

"I'm not going to argue with you now. You're being stubborn and foolish. We'll wait for our brothers to arrive."

"She will have to quit. Her job is too dangerous. We lost Margo. We can't lose Sal."

"I know. I was thinking about it, too. Told her we can talk things through and not to rush all the thinking."

"Good. How was her dad? What was up with him?"

"I don't know. I sensed something about him. I swear he has some magical powers. He took Sal into the other room and explained about her past and something with her mother. They kept the conversation quiet and then she came out with all these questions over dinner."

"Interesting. And you don't know what they discussed? Why would they keep you out of it? Has her father accepted your appointment as one of her mates? What was the discussion about?"

"Not a clue, but whatever it was it got her to ask questions and she seemed more accepting to the truth. Her father did condone the process of mating and the confirmation from the gods that it was her fate and she should accept it. I'm so tired. I could imagine that Sal is feeling pretty damn overwhelmed. She's a sweet woman, tough and passionate about her job, helping people, and putting away bad guys. But she is also stubborn to a fault. I know she won't accept this despite Reggie's and her father's time with her. We'll have our work cut out for us. " Quinn closed his eyes and clasped his hands over his waist.

"I'm going to take the first shift. Eagan and Delaney should get here by morning. We'll talk to Reggie about that conversation Sal had with her father. Maybe he knows more," Angus stated.

"Okay. It will be good to see them, and in regards to Reggie, I'm certain he does know more. I'm just not sure why he hasn't let us in on everything."

Angus felt the tightness in his chest.

"He'll talk to us." He ran his fingers through his hair and took a deep breath then released it.

"It will be good to see our brothers," Quinn said.

"It's been nearly a year. Far too long for us to be apart."

Quinn nodded his head and then closed his eyes and got comfortable on the couch. Angus walked into the other room, away from Quinn and Sal, to make a phone call.

* * * *

Sal was tossing and turning. As tired as she was, it seemed too difficult to sleep with all the crazy thoughts going through her head. She got like this often, especially when she worked a case and wanted to solve it. She would ponder over all the information she gathered and analyze it, come up with a profile, and then hopefully a lead. But this was different. This wasn't a case and this wasn't normal.

She drew the covers back and sat up. She felt hot and thirsty, as she stood up, stretched, and pulled the tank top she wore to bed lower over her belly. She looked around for a robe. She had never really bothered with one before, but with two strange men in her home, ones who could shift to wolves and eat her, she didn't want to feel so exposed. She glanced at the clock. It was four o'clock in the morning. They had to be passed out.

With no luck in finding the robe, she tiptoed out of her room, down the short hallway to the kitchen in only her tank and short shorts. The cool tile felt so good against her hot feel. She wondered why she felt so overheated. It was a cool night outside, maybe opening up some windows might help. She reached for the one in the kitchen and pushed it open as she bent over the sink.

"Not planning on escaping are you?"

She gasped and turned, ready to fight as she made two fists and prepared to defend herself.

Quinn's eyes widened, but he didn't move closer. He kept his distance. She relaxed her stance as she absorbed every glorious ounce of the man. He wore only boxers, black, and he was covered with muscles upon muscles, plus some seriously intricate tattoos.

Her breasts tingled, and her pussy clenched. He sniffed the air, then smiled.

He walked closer. She held her breath as he reached over her shoulder and closed the window. His upper arm, hard as steel, grazed her breast.

She stifled a gasp.

"Don't want to give anyone easy access in breaking in do we?" he asked and winked at her. She closed her eyes, suddenly overcome with desire and her senses in overdrive with the man this close to her. She felt the intensity of his personality, the strength and solidity of his muscles, and of course, his scent. He even smelled manly and desirable. It was so wild, so insane, because she had never sniffed anyone before or felt so in tune to them. She let the sensations wash over her body until she felt a large, heavy hand on her hip. Opening her eyes, she looked up, her head as far back as it could go to lock gazes with him, and he stared intently.

"You smell so good, Sal," he told her. She gulped and gripped the counter behind her tighter. His warm, hard fingers caressed against her skin under the tank top she wore.

"I can't believe you're real. That the gods have granted us a mate."

She went to speak and had no voice. He stepped closer, pinning her body snuggly against the counter.

"You're a pleasant surprise." He leaned forward, his lips inches from her own when she panicked. She lowered her head and moved away from him.

He grabbed her hand, and she turned to look at him.

"You feel it. Don't bother to fight. It's meant to be."

She shook her head. "I don't like change, and this is something I'm definitely not comfortable with." She walked away, her heart aching, her pussy begging her to stay and play with the sexy man behind her, but she couldn't do it. How could she accept such a fate? She knew what she needed to do. She needed to get back to work. She didn't care what Reggie or Benjamin said. Tomorrow, she was going to have the safety and protection of her job, and the entire shield, toughness, and attitude it allowed her to show. She needed that, and nothing anyone said would matter.

Chapter 6

Reggie stared at Sal as she got into the unmarked police cruiser. He glanced at Quinn and Angus, who looked downright ready to kill.

"Sal, I thought we went over everything last night. I thought you understood the seriousness of the situation after speaking with your father."

"Reggie, drive the damn car and get me out of here. I belong working, not with them."

Reggie gave a nod to Angus as Quinn got into the SUV. Angus followed.

He put the car in reverse and headed down the street with the SUV following.

"You do belong with them. You feel the connection, the attraction already."

"I do not," she said, but he watched her cross her legs and turn toward the window. He knew what was happening. Her body was reacting to being separated from Angus and Quinn. It was that strong of a bond.

"The itch, the pain will only increase the further you are away from your mates."

She slammed her hand down on the dashboard. "Stop that. Stop calling them my mates. I'm not a wolf."

He took a deep breath and released it. "They won't leave your side. You heard them. They lost one mate to murder. You seriously think that Angus and his brothers will take a chance like that again?"

"I don't know and I really don't care. I need to do my job. I need to continue investigating and so do you. We have that case from two weeks ago to continue to investigate. We need to meet with the banker. Those two men were found murdered, their savings accounts drained, and no one saw shit."

He gripped the steering wheel tighter. "I know that, and I know who they are. It's a Were pack situation. The two men had a mate that was taken and her body was found weeks ago. There are other detectives investigating. We don't need to do much right now."

"Bullshit. It's my case. I arrived, I'll be the damn human who gets to solve it. This is insane. I'm living amongst all these things, these wolves, wizards, and such and didn't even know it. Now you're telling me these men who were found dead shared a mate who had been abducted and then was found murdered, too? What the fuck kind of laws do you things have that can allow such atrocities to take place?

"Things? We're not things. We have more strength, power, and abilities than any human could ever imagine. There is a hierarchy that has recently entered into renovation. Just take my word for it."

"Take your word for it? How can I do that when you are pushing me toward entering a relationship with perhaps six huge-ass men who can shift into beasts, kill people, tear their hearts out from their throats and who follow leaders who allow mates to be taken from one another? Are you out of your fucking mind? I live to help people like this. I became an investigator so I could catch killers not become part of an association that condones their behavior all behind ignorant humans who live unaware. Then there are wizards. Magi, vampires, and fairies? What the hell kind of fairies? Like Tinker Bell, or annoying little minxes? What?" she asked, raising her voice.

"Humans don't know it, and not wizards. Wizards are rare, just as you, a Magi, are rare, Sal. It's a serious situation and I need you to be rational."

"I am trying to be rational. Believe me I am, but it's too much. I need time to process all of it. I have had these feelings inside of me for as long as I can remember. I've had these dreams, these situations at night that felt more like encounters, like real events. I wondered where they came from, and if I was losing my mind. I started to think the job, the murder investigations and dealing in dead bodies all the time, was getting to me. But then this happens. I shoot two men in the head and they get up and walk away at some point after the police leave. That's another thing. How many people are secretly involved to cover this shit up? It makes me feel on edge and on the defensive. It's a bit shocking, okay? I'm trying, Reggie, but I'm not about to let go of the control and hand it over to men who shift into wolves and want my body to breed more wolves from. Sorry, no can do. I do need a bit more coaxing than that to get me to spread my legs." She crossed her arms and ground her teeth as she stared out the window.

Reggie exhaled and tried to understand. She would need time. Sal was a leader, an Alpha female in all aspects whether human, Magi, or wolf. This was her way and he needed to help her through this.

"Listen, open the glove compartment. There are two clips in there. Reload your revolver with one and replace the ones you have with those."

She eyed him suspiciously.

"Why?"

"Just do it. If you won't let your mates protect you, and if you're insistent that you're going to continue to work, then at least I can prepare you somewhat to defend yourself if necessary."

"What types of bullets are these?" she asked, looking at the clip.

"Silver."

"Why are they wrapped in this stuff?"

"So I wouldn't die handling it."

"What?"

"Silver is very powerful and can kill a wolf. We can't even handle the stuff it's so potent. So please be fucking careful. I know how you like to shoot first and ask questions later."

"I do not." She loaded her weapon.

"Oh really? Tell that to Angus."

Her cheeks turned a nice shade of red and Reggie had to hide his chuckle. Little did she know that there was no fighting the bond between intended mates. Even though it seemed that Sal and Angus would fight it tooth and nail for their personal reasons, once the others arrived, she didn't have a chance. He knew he was jumping the gun, but he had a feeling that Sal would belong to all six Fennigan brothers. He smiled. They were in for a hell of a fight, and she was in for a hell of a ride.

As he pulled the car along the shoulder near the entrance to the main bank, he spotted Quinn driving the SUV around the corner. Even though they would remain out of sight, Reggie knew they were nearby.

They both got out of the car and he locked it up.

"So how do you want to handle this?" she asked him.

"I do all the talking, you do what you do best and read the guy."

"Okay. Let's do this."

"Hey, is that lip gloss you're wearing?" he asked her as they entered the building, passed security, and headed toward the elevators.

"What? Oh, yeah, why?" She slid her finger under her lip as if she forgot she put it on. In fact, she also had an extra button undone on her blouse, which was still not what he would consider risqué, but it was for Sal. She looked good, sexy, and he swallowed hard. He'd known her for years, and she was his cousins' mate and all, but he was a man and he did recognize a sexy, attractive woman when he saw one. It just stunned him a moment when he saw Sal in that way. He was trying to figure out why he felt like this. He looked her over again, feeling something he hadn't felt before. He sniffed the air, then moved closer.

She turned to look at him.

"What the hell are you doing?" she asked softly.

He squinted his eyes and inhaled again. There was something about her scent. It was different.

"Did anything happen between you, Quinn, and Angus last night?"

"No. Why?"

He looked away and then turned back to her as the doors opened.

"You're freaking me out, Reggie. You've never sniffed me before."

"There's something different about your scent. It's very appealing to my wolf, and well—"

She walked out of the elevator, interrupting his sentence as they entered a seating area and main desk. "Hello, we're here to see Mr. Francisco," she told the receptionist.

"And you are?"

"Detectives Fennigan and Santos."

"Is he expecting you?"

"No, but he knows what it's about. Is he inside now? We can show ourselves in," Sal stated.

"Let me just buzz him. He is in a meeting but it should be over by now." The secretary picked up the phone to buzz Mr. Francisco.

Reggie couldn't believe what he smelled. It was Carbarone pack. Someone from the pack was here, and maybe in the office with Francisco.

Sal turned to look at Reggie. He tried to relax.

"Reggie, what's wrong?"

"Nothing."

The doors opened and three men walked out, shaking hands and ending their meeting. Both she and Reggie looked. Reggie recognized Vargon Carbarone and Jaydin, his nephew and an Alpha in his pack.

Reggie felt his hackles rise and had to force his wolf to remain calm. But then Vargon and Jaydin looked at Sal.

"Detective Santos and Fennigan, this is a surprise. I was just ending a meeting with some colleagues. Was there something I could assist you with?" Mr. Francisco asked. Reggie pressed closer to Sal. He placed his hand against the small of her back and she gave him an odd look over her shoulder. He hoped she didn't step away from him. He needed to protect her from these men.

She of course stepped away from him. The stubborn woman. Hadn't she felt the way these men looked her over like their next meal? If they smelled the desirable aroma coming from her scent just as he had minutes ago, then there could be a potential situation here.

"Sorry we didn't call first. We were in the neighborhood and we thought we would give it a shot and see if you could answer some questions for us," Sal said. His concern was protecting his cousin's mate and nothing else.

"I see you're still working the streets, Reggie, thought they'd eat you alive by now," Carbarone said, and then looked at Sal.

"I don't believe we've met. My name is Vargon Carbarone. You're Detective Santos?" he asked as he reached his hand out to her. Reggie went to stop them from shaking hands but Jaydin pressed in the way.

"You're a lucky guy having such an attractive partner." As Jaydin said the words and inhaled closer to Sal, his eyes widened.

Reggie knew that both men smelled her scent. He wished Quinn and Angus had gotten her to begin the mating process so that these men smelled Fennigan pack on her, but they didn't and now both men seemed interested.

Sal suddenly realized who Carbarone was and she stepped a little closer and Reggie had no idea why. She held her ground and gave him the once-over then rolled her eyes.

"Carbarone? How interesting to meet you here. Are you conducting business with Mr. Francisco?" she asked.

Carbarone stepped back, but Jaydin remained staring at Sal, inhaling her scent.

"We're good friends, have been for quite some time. Well, we must be going. Nice to have met you, Detective Santos. Hopefully we meet again."

She watched him walk away and Reggie did the same, taking his eye off of Jaydin a moment.

When Reggie turned back, Jaydin lifted Sal's hand to his lips and leaned down and kissed the top of it. "Such a pleasure to meet you. I hope you don't mind me saying this, but you are quite beautiful, gun and all." He released her hand, smiling and then winking.

Reggie saw Sal's face turn a little red, but she whispered a "thank you" before turning toward Francisco, her eyes back on the purpose of their visit.

"Mr. Francisco, if you don't mind, we have a busy day ahead of us. Could we speak to you in your office? It won't take long," she said, stepping to the side. Francisco waved his hand for her to head in before him, and Reggie watched Carbarone and Jaydin.

"I'll be seeing you around, Reggie," Jaydin said, but it was more like a threat as the fucker flashed his wolf eyes.

"Anytime, Jaydin. Anytime." Reggie walked by them. Before he closed the door, he could hear Carbarone giving orders.

"Not a word, we'll talk in the elevator," Carbarone said. Reggie inhaled then exhaled. He could relax a little right now. Sal was safe and that was what mattered most.

* * * *

"I can't believe this," Carbarone stated aloud with a big smile on his face. He ran his hands over his chin and looked at Jaydin.

"Did you smell her scent? Did you see how lovely she is?"

"How could I not. She was very enticing, just as Luka had indicated."

"I have an idea. That is, if what we both smelled was in fact magic powers. She would make a great mate for you and your brothers, Jaydin. She could be very useful in providing the power and strong arm we need to take over Skylar Pack. You're young, strong, and more than capable of challenging McCarthy for lead Alpha of his pack. This could work out even better and help us legitimize the process through Were law."

"What are the chances that she has some kind of magic blood in her? It could mean anything. She could be a Magi, or a healer, or maybe even wizard. I wonder what she is exactly. What do you think?"

"Slim, but our sense of smell is quite trustworthy. It's more than coincidental," Jaydin said as he started to text on his phone.

"We'll need to confirm and only Torque can assist with this."

"Well, how do you suggest we do that without revealing that Torque is indeed alive?" Jaydin asked.

"I'll think of something. In the meantime find out what you can about her. Make an effort to meet her again."

"It seemed to me that Reggie was quite protective of her."

"Of course he was. She's his partner and he knows what we're capable of."

"He'll challenge me and my brothers for her."

"And you'll accept that challenge. I know you, Jaydin. You want to destroy all the Fennigan Pack members just as I do, and just as my son Luka does. Taking over Skylar Pack is a stepping stone in that direction. Finding Sal, that is just a very delicious bonus. This was more than just coincidence, us meeting her here."

"What about Mr. Francisco? Do you think he'll be able to handle their questions?"

"He doesn't know anything. What we did, we did behind his back so he wouldn't be able to give us up. Mr. Francisco is weak, just like the others, but another asset to my plan to achieve more financial power. Notify your brothers about Detective Santos. I have a feeling that things are going to really start falling into place."

* * * *

"Well, that was a waste of time. Francisco didn't know shit," Sal stated as she and Reggie headed downstairs and out the main lobby.

"I wouldn't exactly say it was a waste of time. I think the man legitimately doesn't know that he's dealing with conniving wolves. As a human, he's unaware of the capabilities Carbarone has."

"Are you sure Francisco is human? He was definitely eyeing me over a lot."

"You're an attractive woman, and apparently that scent on you I've been inhaling all morning is appealing even to humans."

She lifted her sleeve and sniffed. "What scent? You smell something on me? I just got this blouse from the damn dry cleaners."

"No, Sal, it's not on your clothing, it's emitted from your skin, your body, and believe me it is not unpleasant."

He gripped the steering wheel and Sal felt a bit uncomfortable with this conversation. Reggie was her partner, her friend for years.

She turned in her seat to face him. "Okay, spit it out. Explain this shit."

"Okay, it's normal for all Were, all people to carry a scent. It helps differentiate your families, the packs you come from, the bloodline you originate from. It's how we, as wolves, distinguish who is who. You've always had a distinctive scent that was appealing, and sweet. But now, just in the last hours since I left you last night, that scent has deepened and it's hard to explain but it's so damn enticing. It's taking a lot of self-control to not take a closer sniff and even taste your skin."

"What?" She leaned back against her seat. She didn't like the sound of this. It gave her the creeps. All this sniffing and licking. She immediately thought about Quinn and Angus. She sure would like to explore their bodies with her mouth and tongue. She shook her head. "Okay, so why this strong scent now?"

"I think it has something to do with you finding your mates."

"Frigging cool it with that stuff. I do not have mates. I am not a wolf. I will not be beckoned by them to do their deeds as ordered.

Now, onto reality of life. I'm a detective. We're investigating a double murder. What's the next step now?"

Just then dispatch came over the radio. Shots fired, and it was a block from where they were. She reached for the radio and responded. "On route to location…" As she gave the information and they headed down the block, whizzing through traffic, she felt the adrenaline rush. A car chase. Pretty sick in the middle of the city. As they made their way closer, less traffic filled the streets and Reggie slowed down, trying to find the street where the incident was taking place. The call came over the radio. "Black Tempo, tinted windows, license plate number…"

A car slammed into the side of their vehicle. She looked up, saw the make of the vehicle matched the one that dispatch had just alerted all cars to, and then she saw the driver. He had glowing eyes and Reggie yelled for her to get down. He raised a gun and fired. The shots rang out, shattering the glass. Reggie jumped out the driver's side and raised his gun. Sal brushed the glass off her shirt, feeling the scratches to her arm as she crawled from the seat and joined Reggie. Three other men emerged from the vehicle. They were wearing masks. She heard the sirens of the additional backup on their way and then a patrol car slammed into the other car. Reggie pulled Sal to the side, she rolled to the ground, and one man with the glowing eyes ran toward her. She pulled her gun, as he pulled his.

"I'm not going to jail!" He reached for her. She shot him and he practically exploded on sight. She was shocked at the capabilities of silver bullets against werewolves.

"Holy shit, run."

She heard the other men yelling. Reggie fired his weapon and so did the other cops. Two of the three got away.

There were police everywhere and then the sounds of a vehicle skidding to a halt. She looked up as Reggie reached down to help her. She glanced that way, and everyone, including Quinn and Angus, seemed to part as two huge men made their way through the chaos of people.

Her mouth went dry, and her body reacted immediately as Quinn offered her a hand, but her eyes focused on the other two big guys. Both were hard looking, attractive, and very muscular, just like Quinn and Angus. One had reddish-brown hair that reached his shoulders with tattoos on his big-ass biceps. The other had dark-brown hair and looked about ready to kill someone.

"Shit, you have cuts on your arms. What the hell just happened?" Quinn asked as he lifted her up and held her by her shoulders.

"We don't know. The call came over the radio of shots fired, and then as we approached, this car slammed into us," she explained. She tried brushing off her pants and blouse after she placed her gun back into her holster.

"What the fuck you shoot that one with, silver?" the big guy asked, all pissed off and also with a deep Irish brogue.

"They shot at us, Delaney. One was about to shoot Sal, so she shot him," Reggie explained.

"Well, looks like you're a pretty damn good shot like Quinn told us, lassie," the other one said.

"She sure is, Eagan," Reggie replied.

Quinn stared down into her eyes as he caressed her lip with his thumb.

"Dangerous job you have, Salina. I'm not feeling too comfortable with it at all," Quinn whispered. His gaze was intense.

"Let's get this cleaned up. Team Seven just arrived," Angus informed them.

Sal looked away from Quinn and tried to avoid looking at Eagan and Delaney. If these men were Angus and Quinn's brothers, and also so-called mates to her, she might just pass out. They were gorgeous, intimidating, and so freaking huge she felt as if she couldn't breathe. Reggie gave her a little push against her arm. She was shaking and didn't like these feelings that were flowing through her body.

"Who is Team Seven? I've never heard of them, or seen them before," Salina said, trying to get her mind off of the sexy men surrounding her. Then she noticed another five men giving orders. They were all dressed in black, wore dark sunglasses, and had every officer running into position putting up road blocks and blocking people's views of the accident and crime scene.

She couldn't even see their faces, but could tell they were tan, extra large like the Fennigan brothers, and assertive.

"They're here to clean up the mess and make sure the human police don't get involved. It was a robbery pursuit, but the bad guys were wolves," Reggie informed her.

"Holy crap. How come I've never noticed anything like this before?" she asked, staring in awe. Her mind was whirling with so many questions as she wondered how many times this so-called cleanup crew showed up on her and Reggie's incidents.

"Let's find out what we just got shoved into, Sal. I really don't want to spend the rest of the shift fucking around with paperwork."

"It's inevitable. We shot our weapons and I killed that thing," she said.

Reggie chuckled. "Yeah, the fact that the 'thing' exploded on impact from the silver bullet may need a bit more detailed explaining. You get to do the paperwork then," he teased.

"You gave me the silver bullets," she retorted.

"It comes with the territory, Sal. You used them, so you get to explain."

She gave him a mean expression as he walked away. She went to follow but Angus pulled her by her arm.

His hand, huge like a mitt, not only made her feel intimidated but entirely too aroused by his masculinity.

She stared at where his hand was as his brothers gathered close. The four of them inhaled deeply. She saw their eyes glow slightly and so fast she thought she might have imagined it. She swallowed hard. Did they want to touch her, mate with her, or just eat her? How had she pissed them off? This was too complicated. She could foresee the disaster multiple men sharing one woman could cause.

"What the fuck is going on, Angus? How can this be?" Delaney asked as he inhaled deeply while letting his eyes roam over her body. Her nipples hardened, her pussy clenched, and she tried pressing her thighs together. Pulling slightly from Angus's hold did nothing. The man firmly held her.

"It's why we needed you to meet us. Meet our mate, Sal Santos," Angus said, and then Delaney and Eagan looked her body over again as if they could see to her soul and stepped closer to take a better sniff.

"You smell that?" Eagan asked Quinn.

"She didn't have that scent yesterday. This can't really be what I think it is," Angus said aloud, and he didn't seem pleased, which really set her whole "I'm feeling sexy" attitude out the window. Now Angus found her scent unappealing? How could that be? *Why should I care?* She pulled her arm free and stared at him.

"What is it? Reggie noticed something different, too, but he wasn't turned off like you, Angus," she said.

"You mean you don't know, sweetheart?" Delaney asked her, looking peculiar as he did.

"I didn't say it turned me off," Angus added, but she abruptly turned away from him.

"I don't need this. I don't know why you're here but you need to leave. This is a crime scene and Reggie and I have work to do." She shoved by them and back toward Reggie and the patrol officers on scene.

"You've got some explaining to do, Angus," Delaney said to his brother.

"We know as much as you do. We'll wait for Adrian and Brady to arrive, and then we'll know if she's mate to all of us or not."

Sal could hear them talking. She was only a foot or so away, and as she felt her belly tighten and an awareness grow stronger in her, she started to feel panicky. Two more brothers were headed into town. That would make six, and by the looks of Delaney and Eagan, who had just shown up, feeling sexy changed to feeling scared shitless.

Chapter 7

"How the hell can this be happening, Angus? With everything we've gone through, is this another fucking joke by the gods?" Eagan asked, his thick Irish brogue more apparent with his anger coming through.

Angus stared at his brother. Angus, Eagan, and Delaney were leaning against the SUV, waiting for Sal and Reggie to finish up their paperwork after the incident in town. Quinn was with them, so Angus wasn't too worried.

"It doesn't seem to be a joke, but I understand your shock. We're all feeling the same way," Angus replied.

"She sure is good looking, and damn, what a body on her," Delaney said aloud.

"You're telling me. But when she pulled that gun, shot without hesitation, and didn't even flinch at the mess those silver bullets caused, I swear, I was instantly in love with the lassie," Eagan told them. Delaney chuckled. Angus grunted.

"What's with you, brother? Still harboring the thought that you were responsible for Margo's death?" Eagan asked.

Angus shot his brother a dirty look. "No need to discuss it. It is what it is. She's dead," he replied then looked up toward the building where he knew Sal was. His gut clenched with worry. It was a constant concern, an anxious feeling of being out of control.

"Maybe it is a good time to discuss it. Considering we've all been apart for nearly a year's time, I'd say the current situation calls for a bit of chatting," Eagan told Angus.

Angus grumbled a response and pushed away from the vehicle.

"So if you don't want to talk about Margo, then why not explain about how you met Sal? And what's with that name anyhow? Ain't Sal a guy name?" Delaney asked.

"It's short for something," Eagan said.

"It's Salina," Angus told them, and he instantly found the name to be quite pleasant.

"So go on and explain," Eagan said.

Angus told them about the night Sal shot Luka and Centron, and how it seemed they were seeking revenge.

* * * *

"He wants to see you alone in his office," Reggie told Sal as they finished up their paperwork.

"Shit. I thought he left early today. How the hell did he find out I was working?" she asked.

"Sal, please, give me a break. He's our damn lieutenant. Of course he knew you were working and of course he found out because you shot a guy to pieces."

She nearly snarled at Reggie. "He wasn't in pieces. I just ensured that he wouldn't come back from the dead like some other criminals I recently thought I took out."

He chuckled. "Try to hurry along. I'm sure Eagan and Delaney are antsy to get to know their new mate better."

"You are such a jerk. Learning that you're, well, what you are, is freaky enough. But your cousins? Well, they're huge, they're intimidating, and more keep showing up wanting to do whatever it is one does while mating or bonding or whatever. I can't believe that you're finding enjoyment in this. I am losing my mind and my patience. Can't you get rid of them?"

He shook his head. "No can do, sweetie, and the faster you accept your destiny the smoother things will go. I can tell you that they'll take very good care of you, and well, the mating process is very enjoyable and they will keep you very satisfied." He winked.

"Reggie!"

"Besides, once they find out that Jaydin and Carbarone met you today, sniffed you, and that Jaydin kissed you, I'd say you'll be in a heap of trouble with your men."

"Don't you dare do that. Don't tell them about Jaydin. I don't need some overprotective wolfmen to start acting all caveman and barbaric. I can handle Jaydin or any other male that comes sniffing around. Surely, even though I was oblivious to it, I probably got rid of a few of your kind before," she said, her face flush.

"Yeah, I can name a few in this department alone who you knocked down a few notches. But Jaydin Carbarone is different. Don't go falling for that nasty wolf's charms either. He's no good. He was part of the scam to kill your mates' other mate, Margo. He's no good."

"It doesn't matter anyway. I told you before that I'm not doing this the traditional way. I'm my own protector. Always have been."

"Why can't you just let things happen the way they're supposed to happen? You know, nice and smooth instead of rough and chaotic?"

"Ha! I don't do smooth. I'm more like a bumpety-bumpety-bumpety, yahoo, hold-on-for-your-life kind of gal."

He chuckled. "That's part of what makes this so fucking funny."

"What?"

"Just how the Fennigan brothers will react once they find out you met Jaydin."

"Santos!" She heard her name and turned toward the lieutenant's door. Benjamin looked pissed off. She gave Reggie an "oh shit" expression and Reggie turned away, trying not to burst out in laughter.

Nice. Really nice.

She made her way to the office and the lieutenant was there, leaning against his desk.

"Close the door, Santos."

Santos? He is pissed at me.

He looked her over and inhaled deeply then scrunched his eyes together. It didn't sit right. She wondered if he were a wolf, too. She eyed him right back the way he did to her.

He raised his voice. "Don't know how to take a direct order, do you?"

"Well, sir, I was feeling fine—"

"Feeling fine my ass! I told you to take a few days off. Reggie and the other detectives were looking into these two men you shot and killed. It appears that their family is interested in seeking some revenge. Didn't they try to hurt you outside your home yesterday?"

"Well, technically it wasn't their family, and I had that under control."

"Under control? Like today's incident where you fired your weapon again and took out some wolf with silver bullets?"

She swallowed hard. No one was really supposed to know about wolves. Was this a test of some sort? She was pretty sure Reggie and her father warned her about never talking or telling anyone about wolves and supernaturals' existence on earth.

"What?" she asked, staring at him.

His eyes flared. "You know damn well what I'm talking about. You smell like Fennigan Pack. Why is that? What are Angus and his brothers doing in New York?" he asked her.

She didn't feel right about this conversation. Her gut clenched. She suddenly remembered Quinn's words about following her gut, her instincts, and her body. Maybe he didn't mean in this way, but she sure wasn't going to be the one to break the ancient secret of wolves in men's bodies walking the earth.

"Sir, I don't know what you're talking about. I don't know any of those names you mentioned, and wolves? What's this all about?"

He raised one eyebrow up at her and stared at her then inhaled again. Again, she wondered if he was a wolf, and if wolves could smell the scents of one's pack or whatever, could they also sense and smell fear?

"They were there at the crime scene this evening. They showed up right after you and Reggie got the call over the radio. How can you stand here and lie to me?"

"Lieutenant, I don't know why you're so upset about this. About them. If the names of the men you mentioned belong to the friends of Reggie's who showed up, then so be it. Reggie said that his cousins were in town. I really didn't pay attention to them or remember their names. I was too busy trying to get over the fact that I've killed three men in the last forty-eight hours and two of them disappeared from the coroner's office."

He came back around his desk to face her. When he reached out to touch her hand, she felt her own defenses rise in warning. It was odd, but she kind of felt guilty, which was insane.

"Sal, I'm sorry. I didn't mean to interrogate you about these men. First things first, how are you handling everything?"

She took a deep breath and released it. Which was hard to do considering that her lieutenant was holding her hand and caressing her wrist. It gave her the creeps. Staring at Benjamin, her lieutenant and his big brown eyes, dark chocolate hair he liked to slick back, she felt a bit of a sensation to pull away inside of her. It was strange.

"I'm hanging in there. I think I'm handling things well."

He caressed her hand. "Maybe you should take a few days off. Maybe visit your dad, or just do something to take your mind off of things."

He looked her body over, and even though he was a good-looking man, her body didn't react whatsoever. But it did for Fennigan Pack. What the hell?

"I'm good. I like my job and keeping busy doing what I do best makes more sense than taking some time off."

"Sal, these men, the Fennigan Pack, I know they're cousins with Reggie, but their reputations are shady to say the least. They're very violent and barbaric. They come from Ireland and do things way differently than here. I just don't want you to fall for their charms." He pulled her closer and inhaled.

"Lieutenant." She gasped and placed her hands against his solid chest.

"I can smell them on you." His voice sounded so deep, and kind of angry. She pulled her hand from his, and stepped back. What was with his behavior? Why was he bad-talking Reggie's cousins? She wondered what was happening here and figured she needed to end this conversation and get the hell out of his office. If her lieutenant was a wolf, maybe he was from a different pack that didn't like Fennigan Pack? She could understand that if she was dealing with humans. Lots of times humans from one department or state agency had to cross jurisdictions for investigations and people felt like they were getting their toes stepped on. Could this be the lieutenant's problem?

"What do you mean smell them on me? Like their cologne? I shook one of their hands, but that was it. Why are you sniffing me? Are you upset because you think they're here to invade your territory or maybe become part of an inter-jurisdictional investigation?"

He stared at her and gave a smirk, not even close to a smile. "I'm just warning you to stay away from them. They're no good. They'll hurt you. I'm certain they are not here for business and to investigate a crime from Ireland here. It must be personal. Now tell me, how did the meeting go with the banker about the double homicide you and Reggie are working on?"

She wondered what was wrong with her lieutenant and then filled him in on the meeting, but left out her and Reggie's theories on the guys losing their mates to abduction. They were waiting to hear from another investigator, a Were one, working the case who found out about the mates being held for ransom.

"No one was there when you arrived?"

Oh, he wants to know about the asshole father, Carbarone, whose son I shot in the head? Interesting. The lieutenant doesn't know that I know Luka is Carbarone's son. I hope my lieutenant isn't one of the bad guys. That would surely suck.

"Some man by the name Carbarone and another guy, Jaydin."

"Carbarone is a very wealthy, prominent man. Jaydin is just as powerful. You'd like him. He's a fighter and doesn't give up easily."

"My kind of person indeed," she replied.

He smiled. "Well, how about dinner? You must be starving, and since Reggie has his cousins in town, he's probably made plans with them."

"Oh, that's okay. I think I'm going to head home, take a hot shower, and just crash. All the stupid paperwork I just finished made my head feel about ready to explode."

He looked annoyed that she declined. Well, tough shit.

"I see. Well, tomorrow's a new day, and don't forget, I need you and Reggie to attend that dedication ceremony. Invitation only, so let Reggie know he can't bring along his cousins."

He smirked and she gave a half smile. "I'll see if Reggie is still going to attend. Was there anything else, Lieutenant?"

He winked at her. "No, you have a good night, and I'll see you tomorrow. Remember, it's black tie."

"Yes, of course." She exited the office. She grabbed her things and didn't see Reggie around. She waved a good night to those still in the office and headed toward the elevator.

She leaned back against the inside of it as the doors closed. She closed her eyes and took an unsteady breath.

What is my life turning into? I swear these feelings I'm getting, these vibes when people are talking to me is making me feel crazy. Does it have something to do with my powers? Who can I talk to about this? Why do I get the feeling that this ceremony tomorrow is going to turn into a serious situation?

With eyes closed she envisioned the party. She was dressed in a gorgeous, sexy red gown, her hair curled and pressed to one side, the back of the dress bare to right above her ass. She glanced around the room at numerous people and noticed who was human and who was something else. It was strange, but just by looking them in the eyes, she discovered who they really were. She saw their thoughts, felt their fears, their desires, and emotions. She locked gazes with a man, a handsome wolf, and realized who it was.

Jaydin.

The oddest sensation gripped her body and suddenly, out of nowhere she felt a strong, muscular arm wrap around her midsection and pull her back. His body was pressed hard against her own. She felt his erection, could feel his hot breath against her shoulders. She melted into his embrace, knowing, sensing that it was safest here instead of out there amongst all those unfamiliar faces trying to hide who they really were. Then came his lips, hard, yet warm against her neck. He kissed her, then brushed his teeth across her flesh directly over a vein. She shivered, her pussy throbbed, and she nearly moaned aloud. His grip tightened and she was right there, ready to come in his arms just from his movement and the feel of his teeth against her pulse.

The elevator doors opened. She opened her eyes, stunned at how lost she was in her own thoughts when she looked up and locked gazes with Quinn.

He looked so concerned. "Are you okay?" he asked her.

She cleared her throat and ignored the sensations flowing through her body as she pulled off the wall. He inhaled and held her gaze.

"I can ease that ache for you, mate."

She nearly stumbled as she took a step. She was overwhelmed with the desire to throw her arms around Quinn's neck and attack his mouth. She wanted to feel his hands all over her body. She closed her eyes.

"Are you okay?" he whispered against her cheek with his hands on her hips.

"Of course. Why wouldn't I be?" she asked with attitude as she exited the elevator with him right beside her. She needed space, some distance between her and Quinn. She needed to get her head screwed on tight or she was going to just give in to these strong sensations and let these men claim her like they said they were going to do.

"Everything went okay with your lieutenant?" he asked.

"Fine," she snapped at him. Even talking with him this close and her body this much on edge made her shake.

"Good, so we can grab dinner and you can get to know Eagan and Delaney."

She hesitated. "I'm kind of tired. I was thinking a hot shower and bed would be perfect."

"A hot shower and bed with you sounds perfect," he teased, keeping his large, warm hand at the dip in her lower back. She went to give him hell, but he chuckled and she knew he was joking. She hid her smile. It turned out that Quinn had quite an interesting personality as well. She looked at the SUV crowded with all the men. Now how was she going to get her own wild thoughts out of her head while she crammed into an SUV with four of them?

Chapter 8

"Are you certain that she doesn't know who they are?" Jaydin asked Benjamin McCallister.

"Yes, sir. She claims that she only knows them because Reggie introduced them."

"It doesn't seem right. They showed up at the scene of the robbery right as Sal engaged one of the robbers. More than coincidence, I think."

"Well, to me she seemed sincere. But there was something kind of different about her."

"Different, how?"

"I don't know. She always had this scent, pleasant, appealing, but there seemed to be more to it. She had a way about her. It was different. But then again, she had killed three wolves in a matter of forty-eight hours."

"Don't remind me. My cousin Luka is determined to see her suffer. However, I've explained to him that she hadn't known who he was at the time. That she will learn her place and will succumb to our commands. As her Alpha, her mates, my brothers and I will be certain she knows her place."

"Her mates? Are you serious?" Benjamin asked.

Jaydin smiled to himself. He knew that Benjamin had a thing for Sal. Hell, after Jaydin showed his brothers her picture and explained a little bit about her, they, too, were very interested.

"Yes, that's the plan. So here is where you come in."

"Me?"

"Yes, Benjamin, you're going to have to help me get some alone time with her. I was thinking tomorrow evening at the awards ceremony. Why don't you ensure that Reggie is kept busy. I'll take care of the rest. Centron will call you with further instructions."

"And what about Fennigan pack?" he asked.

"They shouldn't be there, but if they show up, they won't stand in the way of our plans. We'll have plenty of our people around. Besides, it could give us an insight into why exactly they have been following Sal. Perhaps they know she is special and maybe they are guards of some sort?"

"If they are, then they'll fail just as they failed protecting their mate Margo. My people will call you with the plan." Jaydin chuckled.

"Yes, Alpha, I understand." Benjamin sounded upset.

Well, tough shit. Sal was going to become part of their pack, and soon enough he would gain an understanding of exactly why she smelled so enticing, and what was it about her that all these Alpha wolves suddenly swarming around her? Perhaps the Fennigan men hadn't learned their lesson?

"Sir, we just got word that Adrian and Brady Fennigan have landed in New York. They're here, too, sir," Stoll, one of his Betas, told him.

Jaydin felt the immediate concern. Why would Angus summon his brothers here? They'd been apart for nearly a year. Carbarone, Jaydin's uncle, had wolves in place to take over certain pack property in Ireland on command. Could they be aware of the mission? He thought about that but then kept thinking about how closely Quinn and Angus had been sticking to Sal.

He needed to get to the bottom of this, and the best way would be by engaging her himself. If the Fennigan men tried to ruin this plan of his uncle's, then they would die just like their mate had, pleading for mercy, giving up her life for theirs.

* * * *

Delaney was trying to get over the reality of the situation and the fact that his mate, a new one, was accessible and right here, yet she dismissed him and his brothers. It was the human side of her, but it was really pissing him off. One look around the room at Quinn, Eagan, and Angus, and he could tell that they were having difficulty with this as well.

Sal crossed her legs and leaned back against the couch cushion.

"So, it's getting late and tomorrow is going to be a long day and night for Reggie and me," Sal stated.

"Late night?" Reggie asked.

She smirked. "Did you forget about the black-tie affair and dedication ceremony?"

"Oh shit," Reggie stated and stood up.

"What's this about?" Angus asked.

"This dedication ceremony for the department. It's a black-tie affair, invitation only, lots of big shots. I completely forgot," Reggie told them.

Delaney turned toward Sal, letting his thigh brush against hers. She turned toward him and held his gaze. He could smell her arousal. She was attracted to his wolf, to him.

"Do you really have to go?" He moved his arm over the top part of the couch above her. She was feminine and gorgeous despite her attitude and tough demeanor. She raised her eyes to him.

"Delaney, not that it's any of your business, but yes, I do have to go. My lieutenant made me confirm my attendance today in his office."

He stared into her eyes. "How long is this event?" He placed his hand on her knee and left it there. Sal's lips parted and her face went flush. He held her gaze. "I could think of a lot better, more enjoyable things we could do for an entire night, right here in your town house," he whispered.

She licked her lips and his cock went so damn hard he wanted nothing more than to lift her up onto his lap and taste her sweet lips.

"Hmmm, as intriguing as that sounds, Romeo, I've got plans. So, I need to start getting ready for bed. I'm assuming that you all made arrangements to sleep at a hotel or at Reggie's tonight?" she asked as she stood up.

Quinn stood up and placed his hands on her waist stopping her from exiting the room. "We're not going anywhere, mate. We'll be right by your side from now on."

"I don't think so," she started to say when Quinn abruptly pulled her against him and covered her mouth and kissed her. Delaney felt his own wolf celebrate the kiss, and as Sal initially resisted and then became putty in Quinn's arms, Delaney looked at his brothers. All of them watched with hunger in their eyes.

"I'll be going now," Reggie whispered and tiptoed out of the room. Delaney heard the door close just as he heard Sal moan into Quinn's mouth. Eagan stood up and caressed her shoulders and back. Sal jerked, pulling her lips from Quinn's as they both panted for breath.

"Why did you do that?" she asked him.

"I couldn't resist any longer, mate," Quinn said and then Eagan caressed her cheek, causing her to turn her face toward him. Eagan smiled. "You are gorgeous, Sal." He leaned forward and kissed her next.

Delaney stood up as Quinn stepped from her side and took his place. Delaney's heart was pounding in his chest. He just couldn't believe that the gods had granted them a second chance, another mate. He was worried about her. He wanted to keep her in his arms and hold her to protect her from any potential harm.

Eagan released her lips and smiled. "Delicious and beautiful," he said.

Delaney reached out and cupped her cheek. She turned to look at him.

"You're too much. All of you," Sal whispered.

"Not too much for you, mate. Just exactly what you need." Delaney touched his lips to hers and slowly took a taste. She was sweet, sexy, and inviting. In no time he felt her arms wrap around him and grip tight when he lifted her up so she would straddle his waist best she could. The kiss grew deeper, wilder as he carried her out of the room and to the bedroom. He knew where it was, could smell her scent strongest in that room and on her bed.

Delaney lowered her down, careful not to crush her as he lay half over her, his thigh between her thighs, separating her legs. He slowly released her lips.

He smiled. "You pack a hell of a punch, Detective."

"I could say the same thing for you and your brothers."

He raised one eyebrow at her. "You didn't enjoy it?"

"I did, but that can't happen again. I'm not ready to just accept this."

"Why the hell not?" Eagan asked as Quinn joined them in the bedroom doorway. Sal looked up and pulled her bottom lip between her teeth then cleared her throat.

"Let me up, Delaney."

He held her gaze and caressed her cheek with one finger as he stared down into her big brown eyes. He played with the buttons on her blouse, ready to undo them and see just how well endowed their mate was.

"And if I don't want to?"

She took a breath and released it slowly. "Delaney, I said I needed time to process this. That means without being pushed or persuaded by use of force."

"Use of force?" Eagan asked as he raised his voice and placed his hands on his hips.

"This is not use of force. We'd never physically hurt you or make you do something you're not ready for." Delaney knew he sounded insulted. He damn well was insulted.

"That's not what I meant when I said use of force. I mean sexual stimulation. Using the physical attraction between us to persuade me to allow you free access to my body, my mind, and my soul." She attempted to move and stand. "Now let me up." She tried pushing up and Delaney held his position momentarily just to let her know he was allowing this as her Alpha. It was an odd thought process. Most women just obeyed his commands. Most people did for that matter. Slowly he rose and reached out a hand to help her. When she was standing on her feet, he wrapped an arm around her waist and looked down into her big brown eyes.

"Can't you try to let it happen? Just let yourself go, even if only for a moment so you can feel our sincerity?" he asked.

She swallowed hard. "I'm trying here, Delaney. This is the closest I've allowed a man to get to me in quite some time. There are four of you in my town house. Three squeezed into my bedroom. It's intimidating for various reasons."

"Like what?" Eagan asked, stepping closer and caressing her cheek. Delaney released her to Eagan, who took her hand, brought it to his lips, and kissed her knuckles.

"This. Like what you just did. I'm not used to that. I'm used to being alone, and handling my life on my own and being independent and coming and going when I want to."

"That only needs to change a little," Quinn stated as he leaned against the doorframe, arms crossed, eyes glued to their mate. Sal stood there and stared at him.

* * * *

Sal didn't know what to do next. Truth was, she was entirely too turned on right now to resist them in any manner. Should she let them have her body? Their kisses were so freaking amazing. No one ever made her feel like this. But six men? Six huge-ass, monster-sized

Alpha males in all sense of the word, wanted to have sex with her and mark her their woman.

Would it be so bad? Would life changing be so terrible?

She felt the lips against her cheek. Then Eagan released her to Quinn. He pulled her into his arms and whispered into her ear.

"Just do me a favor and relax and feel what's happening here. Just listen to your body, and forget everything else just for a moment or two. Please, baby."

He begged in that deep, sexy voice, and it pulled on her heartstrings. She closed her eyes as Quinn kissed along her jaw, her neck, while his hands gently explored her body, and then she felt another person behind her. In her mind she knew it was Eagan. She pictured him. He was so tough, rough looking, and forceful in his personality. She felt her heart race just thinking about what Eagan and Quinn looked like and how appealing their bodies were. She felt the lips against her neck from Eagan. Then Quinn kissed her lips softly, pulling away to tease her jaw before returning back to her lips. He was good at seduction, and she was enjoying him teasing her.

Sal felt the sensations filter through her system. Their scent, cologne, trees, outdoors, heaven. She inhaled and then Quinn kissed her again, shocking her and sending her mind into a scene of its own.

She saw him so clearly. In her mind Quinn was kind, quiet, and intelligent. He had helped to plan the counterattack that day their mate was murdered. He felt such a loss. He had thought he would never feel any love for another person again. Her heart ached for him, and then she saw Eagan.

He had such a strong spirit. He was noble, loyal, and so intense. When she envisioned his wolf, reddish brown just like the color of his hair, she knew it was him in wolf form. It shocked her. She understood what was happening and it hit her suddenly.

I can see who they really are.

Her mind flashed to them making love, naked bodies entwined, and when she realized there was a cock in her pussy and one in her ass as she opened her mouth to take another cock to suck it, she gasped, pulling from Eagan and Quinn.

Stepping toward the door, she held her hand over her chest and saw that her blouse was undone. Her large breasts flowed from the black lace bra she wore, and Quinn, oh God, Quinn's shirt was pulled open. He look wild and hungry.

"Sal, it's okay. You let go. You allowed the power of the bond be free."

She shook her head. She ran her hands over her face and eyes. "I saw you. I saw all of us together. I…I'm sorry, I can't do this." She turned to leave the room and hurried down the hallway, shocked at the emotions she was feeling, just as she collided with Angus. He grabbed her arms and held her tight. He appeared furious, and at first she thought it was directed toward her, but then he looked over her and right to his brothers.

"What have you done?" he asked as he tried buttoning her blouse.

"No, it's okay. Nothing happened. We just kissed." She pulled her blouse lapels from Angus's huge hands.

He looked back down at her. "You're upset."

"No, I'm shocked. I said I needed time to process this. I'm not certain this is what I want."

"You don't have a choice. We are your mates as you are our mate. Get used to it, Salina, there will be no other alternatives." He released her and turned around to leave. He looked back at his brothers, stared at them, but no words were spoken. Eagan followed as well as Quinn.

"I'll sleep on the couch. The others will stay somewhere else for the night," Delaney stated then walked to the couch.

She stood there feeling stupid, out of her mind for pushing away four gorgeous, sexy men who wanted to have sex with her. But there was more to it than sex, even she knew that. Plus, she saw their minds, their personalities for who they were. If what she saw was true, then Quinn and Eagan were amazing men, and any woman would be blessed to have them as her men.

So why can't I?

Sal turned around, her blouse moving gently behind her as she walked back to her bedroom. She closed the door and covered her face with her hands.

I'm making a mess of things. I'm hurting them, and they've already suffered so much. But why do they want me? Why is this our destiny? What is it that they want from me? Show me. Let these powers or whatever they are be explained to me and released.

I need proof because once I have sex with six different men who can shift into wolves on a snap of their fingers, I'll never be the same again, and no man will ever want me. That's a huge risk for something I don't even know is real or exists.

Show me, damn it. Just show me.

Chapter 9

"What's the plan?" Jaydin asked as he fixed the bow tie to his designer tux. His brothers Jett and Jeremiah stood there already dressed for the event in their tuxedos as well.

Jaydin ran his hand through his blond hair, slicking it back. "What do you think?" he asked his brothers.

"You know you look good," Jett told him as he fixed his diamond cuff links.

"The woman doesn't stand a chance. She'll be throwing herself at us before the end of the night," Jeremiah added.

"Don't be too cocky with this one, Jeremiah. Sal is a cop, a homicide detective. She shoots first and asks questions later. That kind of tough attitude makes her dangerous in many ways," Jaydin responded.

"I like tough. If she's an Alpha like Uncle Vargon believes, then she will be good enough for the three of us. Have we identified her bloodline yet?" Jeremiah asked.

His brother was cocky and a bit overaggressive with women. Jaydin hoped that he could keep his cool at the event. The last thing they needed was for a situation to occur and a fight to break out.

"Torque will be in the vicinity. He believes he'll be able to identify her pretty quickly even if she covers her scent and powers with some kind of magic."

"That's one thing that bothers me. What if she uses magic on one of us?" Jett asked.

"Don't piss her off and she won't. Just be your calm, debonair self, Jett, and Sal will fall for it," Jaydin replied.

"You met her one time for under a minute, how the hell would you know her response to us?" he asked.

Jaydin turned to look at his brothers. "She is meant to be ours. To mate with a Magi, or whatever she is, will give our pack extra power. Other packs, weaker ones, like Skylar pack and that pussy Alpha McCarthy, will give up easily once he knows what we possess. She'll be ours and it will be another added defense against the Circle's response or even attack."

"I'm not too confident about your choice of women. You always go for the model types with no brains," Jeremiah added.

Jaydin smirked. "For an easy fuck, you bet I do. But for a mate, I won't accept anything but perfection." Jaydin scrolled down his phone and then handed it to Jeremiah and Jett. After Jaydin showed his brothers her picture and explained a little bit about her, they, too, were very interested.

"This is Sal?" Jett asked. A smile formed on his face and his eyes looked about to change to his wolf eyes. Jeremiah licked his lips.

"A tasty-looking morsel indeed. How the hell could she be a detective?" Jeremiah asked.

"She won't be for much longer. The three of us will see to that," Jaydin stated firmly, and Jett and Jeremiah chuckled.

"Let's go," Jeremiah said.

"Patience, brother. Remember that this is a mission, and with a woman as lovely and enticing as Salina, we are not going to be the only men and wolves interested."

Jeremiah growled low. Jett did the same. Both men showed their wolf teeth.

"I'll kill any wolf or man that stands in the way," Jeremiah said.

"Definitely," Jett added. Jaydin nodded in agreement.

"Be ready. It may come down to that."

* * * *

"I'll take care of her. It will only be about four or five hours for the event," Reggie told Angus as he waited for Sal to get ready.

"We'll be there," Quinn told him.

Reggie squinted his eyes. "But how? It's an invitation-only event and all tickets sold out months ago."

Angus smiled.

"We're resourceful wolves, and we won't leave our mate unattended for long," Quinn added.

"Are you all going to be there?" Reggie asked.

"Yes. But no worries, lad, we're fixing on ensuring our woman's safety incognito."

"Sounds good. I'm certain everything will be fine. It's a charity event. What could possibly be dangerous about that?" Reggie said as Eagan whistled long and low. They all turned around and there stood Sal dressed in a red slim-fitting silk dress that hugged her curves and had a long, high slit up the right side. She looked like a fashion model.

"Hot damn, Sal, you're gorgeous," Reggie said, his eyes landing on her abundant cleavage and bare shoulders. It was strapless and showed the definition in her arms and shoulders. When she twirled around, he saw how low cut the back was and knew she wasn't wearing any bra.

Quinn and the others growled low. Reggie swallowed hard, raised his hands up, and stepped away from Sal. She in return placed her hands on her hips and gave the Fennigan men a dirty look.

"Cool it," she reprimanded.

* * * *

Angus tried to calm his beast. Their mate was stunning, an absolute sex symbol with a body his wolf and the man in him craved to take a taste of. But he resisted the emotions, the possessive feeling he had about her. He wanted her safe, and only his brothers, not him, could keep her safe.

"You look beautiful," he told her. She looked him over and nodded her head.

"Thank you."

She reached for her purse, and when she bent down, he saw the way the silk, red fabric revealed her long, tan, toned thigh. His cock hardened to a point of being painful.

"Sal, you look amazing, baby. I want you to be careful tonight. Remember what we discussed about the scent, about your appealing"—he looked her body over, his eyes roaming over her chest—"everything," Quinn told her.

"Listen, I'm a grown woman who knows how to handle herself."

Quinn leaned forward and kissed her on the mouth. She stepped away, panting, looking so damn aroused even Angus felt his brother's arousal and need. All of them did.

"I need time to digest it all and decide what I want. Please don't push me." She moved around to the other side of the couch, right into Eagan.

Eagan took her hand and brought it to his lips. "Lassie, you're perfection. If time is what you want, then time is what we'll give you. We're not going anywhere." He released her hand.

Delaney was there to run a hand down her arm and hold her gaze. They could all smell her arousal, her attraction to them. It was making Angus crazy with need and desire. To see his brothers feeling so compelled to have her, mark her as their mate, was intense. How were they going to let her leave them even for a short period of time? They would need to position themselves accordingly in the venue. He wouldn't let her out of his sights.

"You are lovely, mate," Delaney said, and then cupped her cheek, leaned forward, and kissed her softly.

"We need to go," she replied, sounding breathless, and Reggie opened the door, leading her out of the town house.

* * * *

"I can't believe this. This is not normal or right at all. We should be in bed with our mate making love, marking her, securing the bond, and covering her with our fucking scent," Delaney said, running his fingers through his hair. He was so fucking irate.

"That's why I kissed her thoroughly. My scent, Fennigan scent, should last for a sufficient enough time to let any wolf with a fucking brain know to stay clear," Quinn said.

Delaney looked at him and smiled. "Let's get changed. I don't want Sal out of our sight for too long. My wolf is antsy and I don't like the feelings I have right now."

"Neither do I. Let's go," Quinn said, and they all exited the house to prepare to infiltrate the dedication party undetected but ready for action if necessary.

* * * *

Sal was feeling restless, uneasy, and guilty. It was as if she was missing something, a part of her, or there was this empty, lost feeling. Even her pussy ached as if it needed attention, but she couldn't understand why. It was the strangest feeling. It wasn't arousal or need for sex, it was as if something was missing nearby. She couldn't understand it, and then she spotted Eagan.

She swallowed hard because he was standing near a column, looking sexy and relaxed with a drink in his hand, diamond cuff links shimmering in the candlelight and a look of hunger in his sparkling blue eyes.

He held her gaze, looking her body over from afar, and she felt it.

Her pussy relaxed and oozed some cream, making her shift her standing position and try to regain an understanding of the conversation in front of her. The three men, two of whom couldn't seem to focus on anything but her breasts, were talking about changes in the department and special assault teams being trained for the increase in gangs and drug-related homicides. They mentioned Task Force Eight and a team leader by the name of Lawkins. She remembered hearing about the guy Blaise Lawkins. He was a real hard-ass military type.

"You've done an exceptional job in the field, Sal. Your reputation is impressive," an assistant to Commissioner Brady, Toby Lions, stated.

"I appreciate that, sir. It's been a hell of a few weeks," she replied.

He placed his hand on her upper arm, giving it a squeeze. "Please call me, Toby. There's no need for formalities, Sal." He winked at her and Reggie chuckled.

Sal smiled. "Of course, Toby. Thank you."

"I think that Lawkins's team will be perfect for the position. They're supposed to be here tonight," Toby added.

"I don't believe I've ever met them," she stated, trying to keep the conversation going, but her eyes kept darting toward Eagan.

"If you met them you would know it. They're pretty noticeable, to say the least." Toby chuckled then took a sip from his drink. Reggie started talking about some case and Toby added a few comments, but his gaze kept falling on her breasts and her mouth. It was getting awkward.

"Will you excuse me a moment?" She smirked at Reggie as she walked away from the men and toward the champagne table. As she reached for a glass, she heard a familiar yet strange voice behind her. She immediately knew it was a man, and as she turned, glass in hand, she looked up to see Jaydin Carbarone.

The man looked absolutely gorgeous. His blond hair was slicked back. His brown eyes zeroed in on her lips, not her breasts, and she was amazed.

"Detective Santos, so nice to see you here." He reached close by her to take a glass of champagne.

"Jaydin Carbarone, I'm surprised to see you here." She stepped away from the table and closer to an area where there were various seats and couches.

"Why is that?" he asked.

She looked him over. The man was definitely attractive and she wondered what he wanted. "Not sure. You just don't come across as a philanthropist."

"My family and I are very involved in humanitarian affairs and believe that the local law enforcement organizations need the assistance necessary for ensuring the safety of our communities."

She looked at him, and he held her gaze, inhaled, then seemed to scrunch his eyes together. She looked away from him a moment and saw two other men watching her, looking her body over, and it gave her the creeps.

"That's impressive, Mr. Carbarone, and very kind of you and your family. What type of businesses are you involved in again?" she asked. Being a detective made her a great interrogator, and right now her gut instincts were warning her to tread carefully.

"Please call me Jaydin." He placed his hand on her lower back and guided her toward a set of long couches that had two sides.

His fingers felt cool and hard.

"Shall we sit a few minutes? I'd love to get to know a little more about you, too, Miss Santos."

She walked with him and sat down on the long couch. "Feel free to call me Sal, since we're not being so formal," she replied.

"Who started the name Sal for you?" he asked.

"I did when I was a very little girl." She crossed her legs and her dress parted, revealing all thigh. She probably should have sat on the right, but it was too late now. Jaydin looked her thigh over and then winked at her.

"So you didn't like your full name? It's Salina, right?" he asked and took a sip of champagne.

"Yes. I guess you could say I was pretty independent and a bit of a feminist right from the start. I liked Sal better. It's tough, assertive."

"Like you?" he asked, holding her gaze. Her belly quivered just slightly. He was an attractive man and her body definitely reacted, but nothing like her body reacted to Angus, Quinn, Delaney, and Eagan.

"I suppose. So tell me about your family's business. What exactly do you do, Jaydin?" She took another sip from her champagne glass.

"Well, personally, I'm into business dealings, you know, revamping companies that are going under and investing in potential money-making ventures."

"So risks and high stakes is your thing?"

He let his eyes roam over her body and he held her gaze intently. "The greater the risk, the more stimulating the anticipation."

Her cheeks warmed. This guy was slick. Too fucking slick for her liking. She chuckled and took a sip of champagne and looked around the room.

"Are you laughing at me?" he asked.

She spotted Quinn giving her the evil eye and looking about ready to explode. She turned away from him. Half of her wanted to pretend to like Jaydin and use it as an opportunity to keep the Fennigan men at bay, keep her in control of who she was intimate with or not, but she wasn't a woman who played games or led men on. She didn't feel comfortable with Jaydin, and for some reason she thought that pissing off the Fennigan men might be a very stupid thing to do.

"I am laughing at you and your line. Please tell me that you haven't actually been successful with it before?" she asked him.

He chuckled and smiled as he leaned back and looked around the room.

"Actually I have been very successful with that line. This is the first time I've crashed and burned."

"Well, I'm glad to be the one to burst your bubble. If you'll excuse me, I think I'm going to grab a bite to eat before the champagne goes to my head." She stood up and Jaydin did, too. Just then two other men, the creepy ones, walked over.

"Oh, Sal, before you go, I'd like you to meet my brothers. This is Jett and Jeremiah."

Sal felt her whole body tense up, especially as Jeremiah, the one with the ruff along his chin and an evil look in his eyes, gazed over her breasts. She shook their hands, being sure to be polite as they stepped in her space and sniffed deeply.

Jett's eyes grew darker, and so did Jeremiah's.

"It's nice to meet you. I didn't realize that you had brothers, Jaydin. Are you two in business as well?" she asked. She couldn't believe it, but as she touched their hands to shake them, she felt such an overwhelming sense of evil. In her mind she saw flashes of different things. Things she couldn't be sure were real. There were wolves, there was a lot of blood, there was a woman screaming in pain. She thought about Angus. It was so strange.

"We sometimes work together," Jett stated. "Jaydin does a lot of the legwork. I enjoy playing more often than not." He licked his lower lip.

She felt that uneasy feeling intensify and knew she needed to vacate the little circle of men.

She chuckled and glanced at Jaydin.

"I guess he likes to use lines, too, huh, Jaydin?" she asked, and Jaydin glared at his brother after he winked at Sal.

"Well, if you'll excuse me. I need to mix and mingle, and go see my lieutenant. It was nice meeting the three of you. Enjoy the event."

She walked away and could feel their eyes upon her. She also felt this tingling sensation that made her turn to the left, and there stood Eagan. Then she got another odd sensation and looked around the room and spotted Vargon Carbarone talking with a few men. One in particular looked at her, and she felt something almost sting her skin. Her mind went blank. She didn't know what was happening to her.

She sought out Eagan. She wondered why. It was like she found safety or support in him.

She swallowed hard and bypassed Eagan, knowing that she shouldn't because she was consumed with so many emotions right now, never mind the experience she just had with Jaydin and his brothers. She wasn't certain if they were premonitions, her gut leaning more toward believing what she saw when she shook their hands were facts. They were evil, criminal men. She wrung her hands together and headed toward the ladies' room, not looking at anyone and just needing a moment to herself. As she rounded the corner, she bumped into a wall of steel. It was a man. He gripped her hips and she gasped, not just from the shock of bumping into him, but from the electrifying charge that went through her body and straight to her soul. He had wide shoulders, covered by a crisp white dress shirt, and he was wearing a kilt.

Holy fuck!

Her breasts swelled, her pussy ached, and her legs felt like they would give out momentarily.

"This a hell of a way to run into my mate, lassie. No wonder my brothers are in a huff right now. You're fucking gorgeous," he said. His thick Irish brogue and use of the word "fuck" so freely aroused every inch of her flesh. Never mind how huge and warm his hands felt as they squeezed her hips. Every ounce of her was sexually charged as if his touch flicked on a light switch.

"Who are you?" she asked, her voice quivering as the man in the Irish kilt pulled her against him and pressed her to the wall in the hallway.

His ocean-blue eyes locked gazes with hers and her lips parted, reminding her to breathe and gain some control. This close up she could see the definition in his cheekbones and his neck. Were those tattoos climbing along his neck at the edge of the collared shirt?

"The name's Adrian Fennigan, love, I'm one of your mates, and I must say, the gods sure as shit have got their fucking act together this time. Damn, we're a lucky bunch." His hands roamed over her ass, squeezing her against his body. When he cupped her cheek with his large, thick hand, she felt so feminine and aroused. She held his gaze, unable to speak. This was the fifth brother.

"Ah, I see you found her before I could. Good job, Adrian." She heard the other voice and turned to the left as Adrian eased his hold slightly. She locked gazes with another tall, large, sexy man in a tux. He winked at her, green eyes twinkling with pure mischief.

"Hey, beautiful, the name's Brady. A pleasure meeting you." He stroked his hand down her arm, giving her instant goose bumps. She needed to calm her breathing. Brother number six was on the scene and she felt about ready to faint.

"Are you feeling okay, lassie? Those assholes didn't upset you, did they?" Adrian asked her, and now Brady looked concerned. She shook her head as she absorbed the sight of brother number six, Brady. His reddish-brown hair was similar to Eagan's. But his eyes were green as emeralds and his face absolutely gorgeous.

"Can you please release me? I'm fine," she told Adrian, looking up toward his firm face. The man was a walking fantasy. Her pussy leaked as his strong muscular arms released her. He gave her a wink.

"Can't promise I won't be grabbing a hold of you again real soon. You're just too fucking perfect." He was hard, and his use of the word "fuck" wasn't vulgar but arousing and sexy. She sensed his fierce personality like that of a warrior or fighter. Same with Brady as she smoothed her dress down with her hands and took a deep breath and released it. Both men stared at her and kept real close.

"What are you doing here?" she asked, now somewhat on the defensive. Did Angus arrange this? Were all the Fennigan brothers here as spies?

"We came to meet you. Heard you would be here tonight and we got off our jet about an hour ago. How about we grab a drink and something to eat and you can tell us all about yourself?" Brady asked.

"No, I don't think so. You can tell Angus and the others that I'm not interested right now. I said I needed time to process everything. Showing up here, being a bunch of paranoid bullies, is not exactly a way to win a woman's trust. Now if you'll excuse me." She started to walk toward the ladies' room, but Adrian stopped her. He pulled her into his arms and held her gaze.

"You got spunk, Sal. I fucking love it." He covered her mouth and kissed her.

She couldn't believe it. As annoyed as she was at the fact that this man, sexy as damn hell, dressed in a kilt, took what he wanted from her and spoke his mind, it completely turned her on. As his tongue explored her mouth and he turned her away from the wall, she felt the second set of hands on her hips then lips against her back and shoulders. She shivered, but Adrian continued to explore her mouth, and she was kissing him back. The man had her weak in his arms, and these two men touching her at once set her body into instant flames. The visions hit her simultaneously as her body spasmed, releasing cream from her cunt.

Adrian was indeed a warrior, a fighter to the end, a real badass who sought revenge on his previous mate's murderer. He cared for the woman, although they weren't intimate. He regretted that because he had strong, deep feelings for her. But he hid them well. He wished he had been there to help her fight against the evil ones. The man had killed many to save those in power as well as innocents. He was noble, like a soldier should be.

Brady was wild, strong-spirited, and he didn't take a liking to orders or rules. He was the black sheep in some aspects, or in this case, black wolf. He was naughty, wild, and he, too, sought revenge for his mate's killers. But both of them projected emotions of protectiveness and possessiveness, and she felt the power, the strength of it. She was in awe and almost wished she would be the receiver of such depth of dedication, possessiveness, and care. But she wasn't. She was a means for their packs to continue to dominate and rule.

Spread your legs and bear our children, for numbers rule the kingdoms.

She pulled away, causing Adrian to stop kissing her as they both caught their breath.

"Fucking delicious." He pulled her back against him as he caressed a hand down her ass.

"Please stop this. You can't just kiss me like that."

"Like this?" Brady asked, cupping her cheeks and kissing her next. Adrian released her but kept a hand on her waist as Brady devoured her moans. Before long she was holding on to him, and he was cupping her breast and pressing his thigh between her thighs. She realized things were moving out of control pretty damn fast and she pulled from him. He hugged her to him and squeezed her breast, letting his finger graze back and forth across her nipple.

"So tasty." Brady rubbed his thumb along her lower lip to fix her lipstick.

"Are you two out of your minds? Release me, please," she said, and Brady held her gaze and stepped back. She fixed her dress and took another breath before looking at both men.

"I need to use the ladies' room."

"We'll be right here, lassie," Adrian stated.

"Don't be. I said I needed space, that goes for you two as well." She pushed the door to the ladies' room open and entered. She went to the vanity where a long mirror stood for women to check out their makeup and hair. She stared at herself in the mirror. Swollen lips, flushed cheeks, full breasts, and aching cunt. She looked incredible. She felt amazing and so ready to have sex.

She closed her eyes and imagined them having their way with her. She knew they would be passionate lovers, licking, sucking, fucking every one of her holes. *Holy shit, I've lost my ever-loving mind.* She covered her belly with her hand, almost feeling the quivering sensation penetrate from below her skin and the fabric of her dress. She took some deep, steadying breaths. These were the kind of men women fantasized about. Hell, Adrian's Irish brogue was thick and hard. She wondered if he was naked under that kilt.

She could let him in the bathroom, lock the door, and they would both lift their skirts. He could fuck her right here against the vanity.

She growled and shook her head, trying to clear the horny thoughts.

She had never thought about sex so much in her life. But since the Fennigan men arrived, she'd thought of how it would feel to have them touch her, possess her body, and just plain fuck her brains out in some wild sex fest.

She could do it. They were each so damn stunning and macho. Their deep brogues. Their thick, large muscles and hard-ass attitudes were all a major turn-on to her.

But she couldn't let go. She couldn't be sure it was right and that these feelings would last forever. She just kept thinking that if she had sex with six huge-ass men like the Fennigan brothers, then she would never be the same again, and no other man would ever want her if the Fennigan men got tired of sharing the same woman.

Son of a bitch! What the hell am I going to do?

* * * *

"*So what do you two think?*" Quinn asked Brady and Adrian through their mind link.

"*I think she's fucking gorgeous,*" Adrian stated.

"*I think we need to get her out of here and to the nearest bed. My cock is so fucking hard and my wolf desperate to claim her it's crazy,*" Brady added. They all chuckled.

"*Join the fucking club, brother. We've been feeling that way since day one, but our special little lassie isn't one to let her guard down and accept her fate,*" Eagan said.

"*I can convince her. Just give me ten minutes and it will be done,*" Brady said, all cocky. They laughed.

"You'll just piss her off. She's tough," Delaney said.

"She needs protection. Get your dicks off your minds and focus on her security. I don't like that Jaydin and his brothers sought her out. Jaydin is interested and so are his brothers," Angus interrupted.

"Then we fucking kill them," Adrian said.

"No. We can't and you all know it. Calm the fuck down and stay on guard. Give Sal her space. We'll talk more with her later," Angus ordered.

"Yes, sir," Adrian said. Then he and Brady smiled before they exited the area.

* * * *

"Where did she go?" Jeremiah asked Jaydin as they looked around the dining area for Sal. She was absolutely stunning, but she didn't seem interested in Jaydin, him, or Jett. It kind of pissed Jeremiah's wolf off a bit. Then of course he thought he scented Fennigan Pack on her. Sure enough, the fuckers were all over the place.

"I don't know where she went. Last I saw her enter the hallway over there and then Adrian and Brady Fennigan walked out that way. I can't believe the six of them are here. I wonder why," Jaydin said, taking a sip from his wineglass.

"I hope they're not interested in Sal, too. What if they scented the same thing we did and now they want her for the same reasons we do, to secure their pack's power?" Jett asked.

Jayden looked pissed. "I don't like this. Let's grab her, Jaydin, and take her out of here and see what Torque has to say. It may be our only opportunity. I don't know about you, but my wolf wants a taste of her," Jeremiah told his brothers.

"We stick to the plan. Torque is in the vicinity and should be making contact with her shortly. Let's sit tight and see if we can get a visual. If we can get her alone, and quietly, then we do it and get to know her," Jaydin said.

But Jeremiah was more of a take-charge wolf. He felt compelled to find Sal, pull her into one of the private rooms off-limits to guests, and take that taste he yearned for.

"Jeremiah, please stick to the plan," Jaydin said, looking firm and then walked away.

"What are you thinking?" Jett asked.

Jeremiah looked around them. He locked gazes with Angus Fennigan.

"I think Fennigan Pack wants her, too, and that isn't happening."

* * * *

"Yes, sir, it is a wonderful party and celebration. The dedication ceremony was so beautiful," Sal stated to Benjamin as he talked to her about the event and showed her around the venue, pointing out some big shots and people who contributed financially to the event.

"Why are Vargon Carbarone here, and his nephews and son?" she asked Benjamin.

He turned to look at her, seemingly surprised by her question. "Mr. Carbarone has been a great contributor to the local law enforcement agencies around the state. As a matter of fact, he has financially backed some of the new programs being enforced in the department."

"Really? Is he legit?" She realized how that came out so abruptly. She paused as they walked and looked up at Benjamin. "I'm sorry. That didn't quite come out the way I meant. What I mean is that he seems so pompous and stuck up."

"And his nephews, Jett, Jaydin, and Jeremiah? How were they?" he asked.

"I don't know what you mean."

"Sure you do, Sal. They were monopolizing your time for a while near the sofa earlier. How did they seem to you?"

"Stuck up," she replied and then took a sip of her wine.

"But you found them to be attractive, did you not?"

She gave him an annoyed expression. "I don't think any sane woman wouldn't find the majority of men around this event to be attractive. In fact, I don't recall ever being at such an event where the men were so charismatic and charming."

"You poor thing. Then you just haven't been out to the right places. Jett, Jeremiah, and especially Jaydin are very sought-after bachelors. If you want my honest opinion, they are safer, and a lot better choice for you than one of those Fennigan brothers. I don't even know how they got invitations to come in here," Benjamin said.

"Well, I don't date, so there really isn't anything to consider between them."

He looked her over. "Sal, you are very beautiful and have so much to offer the right men."

"Men?" she asked, feeling her own belly do a series of flips.

"Look around you. Haven't you noticed the multiple partners? There are multiple men with one woman. See over there. And how about right there to the right?" He was pointing out these people who indeed looked as though they were in a relationship.

She watched one woman smile as one man kept his hand on her knee. Another had his hand resting on the back of her neck using his finger to stroke her skin, and the third sat beside her on the chair holding her hand. All three men were touching one woman. Something stirred deep within her heart and soul. She felt it, like a realization of some sort, when suddenly she felt the block, like a wall of darkness to cover her inside and out. She looked up, just as a man—tall, light skinned, handsome, and determined—approached. Something wasn't right.

"Hello, Troy, how are you?" Benjamin asked as the man with the dark hair and almost similarly dark eyes stared at Sal. He smiled, but it didn't reach his eyes. She could tell he was pretending.

"Nice to see you again, Benjamin. How are you?"

"Very good. Please meet one of my detectives, Salina Santos." Benjamin introduced her and the moment she touched hands with Troy, she felt a surge of energy filter through her. In defense, a wall of darkness covered her.

His eyes widened as he pulled his hand away. "Interesting."

"What's interesting?" she asked, catching him off guard.

"I was going to say that I'm surprised you're involved with law enforcement. I could have sworn that someone pointed you out and said that you were a designer." He looked her body over, and it gave her the creeps. She wondered what he wanted. She felt uneasy about being this close to him and didn't know why. She followed her gut instincts.

"Well, I'm not, but I do need to start mingling and catch up with Reggie. It was nice meeting you. And, Lieutenant, I'll see you tomorrow at work." She said good-bye and off she went, making her way toward the back area and an open balcony. Before she could open the door, Jeremiah appeared.

* * * *

"Well, what do you think, Troy?" Jaydin asked as he joined Torque, who was going by the name of Troy to remain undetected. He also wore a disguise just in case.

"She is indeed special. I would need a better sample of her, but from what I could gather before some sort of magic encased her body and blocked me, she is indeed of the Magi, and perhaps even a wizard, too. Quite interesting, because I couldn't scent who was in her bloodline or who her parents were. That's a place to start to know how powerful she may be. I'll work on that now," Troy stated.

"Good, my brothers and I will work on getting Sal to come home with us, or at minimum, get together for dinner tomorrow night."

* * * *

"Looking to get some fresh air? I'll join you," Jeremiah said as he placed his arm around Sal's waist and used his other hand to push open the wooden door. Sure enough there was a large balcony that overlooked the gardens down below.

Sal panicked slightly as she locked gazes with Jeremiah and those dark eyes that freaked her out.

She planted her feet so he couldn't pull her further away from the doorway, her only escape if necessary.

"Actually, I was looking for someone. I didn't mean to head out here. I should get back inside."

He pulled her closer and brought her to the balcony. Placing his large body behind her, he caressed her arms and inhaled her scent.

"I wanted to be alone with you. It's too crowded in there for us to talk."

She turned in his arms despite the powerful way he surrounded her. Physically, she knew she would be no match for the man whom she assumed was a wolf as well. She wished she had her gun, and then thought better of it. Reggie was right. She did tend to shoot first and ask questions later, especially when dealing with wolves. She looked up into his eyes as he zeroed in on her lips and breasts.

"Could you step back please?" she asked him politely.

He reached up and cupped her cheek. "In a moment, there's something I need to do."

It happened so quickly. His mouth was on hers, smothering her pleas for him to stop. His arm was so incredibly strong that he held her neck hard enough that it ached, and she knew he was stronger than any human ever. When he pressed her firmer against the balcony wall, she tried to push away from him, she even kicked him, but it was like kicking iron, and it hurt her instead of him.

She never felt so defenseless and vulnerable in her life. It scared her and made her realize how dangerous wolves could be, Fennigan brothers included. She attempted to close her mouth and block his tongue from exploring, but his hold tightened, making her nearly lose her breath.

He stepped away from the balcony, still holding her tight, and she maneuvered out of his grasp the moment his hand plastered over her ass.

"Stop it!" she yelled. He reached for her and she struck him in the face. He grabbed her by her wrist, and she struck him again, this time with a right hook to his face. It didn't seem to faze him one bit and she felt fear consume her. She was out of her league with this guy. All her training, years of defending herself on the streets when necessary, wasn't a match for a wolf's strength.

She was angry as she clenched her teeth and he laughed at her. "You'll learn your place. Like in my bed with me between your legs."

She spat at him and went to fight him off using everything she had when she felt the strike to her chest and shoulder. She would have fallen, but Jeremiah held her by her hair now and pulled her back against him. She cried out in pain and went to swing but he was so quick he grabbed her other arm and now pulled them behind her back. The move caused her breasts to push forward, nearly popping from the silk garment.

"What are you doing? Let go of me now. Let go!"

"Taking a taste of what will soon be mine." He covered her mouth, kissing her.

"I don't think so." The deep growl of a voice came from out of nowhere. It was Brady, and it was as if the he'd leapt up onto the balcony from the gardens. Jeremiah pulled from her lips but still held her firmly in his arms. She shoved away from him as his grip loosened and he prepared to physically fight Brady.

She glanced to the right to look at Brady as Jeremiah's eyes turned a glowing yellow, confirming his wolf abilities. A strong arm wrapped around her waist as Brady stepped forward, showing his own wolf. She went to resist the hold until Adrian whispered against her ear.

"Are you okay, mate?"

She nodded her head, and relief hit her body, nearly making her lose her ability to stand, even though she felt her wrists stinging and knew they would be red and bruised in no time. Her chest and shoulder felt incredibly sore as Adrian's arm wrapped across her front, holding her snuggly and protectively as he inched her back further away from Brady and Jeremiah. The two men circled one another slowly. It was the craziest scene. They growled low, on the edge of either shifting to wolves or fighting with fists. She was shaking.

"Take a hike, Brady. I'm busy with my woman," Jeremiah said.

Brady chuckled. "Not yours. She's ours."

Jeremiah widened his eyes and took a step toward Brady. "No fucking way. We saw her first. My brothers and I are staking a claim."

"Go to hell!" Sal yelled out.

Adrian's arm tightened around her midsection. "Mind your mouth, lassie, and let Brady handle the little cub."

Jeremiah snarled at Adrian. Adrian chuckled, egging him on. These men were fearless and wild. She felt her body warming and calming in Adrian's embrace, but then Jeremiah growled, baring his long, sharp teeth. It was the wildest, queerest thing she had ever seen. His face mixed between wolfen and human. It was like magic, and as she thought that, she felt a tingling sensation in her core.

"This isn't over. That wasn't my last taste of her either." Jeremiah fixed his tie and headed out the door, closing it behind him.

As Brady turned to look at her, he appeared angry and on edge. His eyes still glowed a deep yellow green. He looked her over and then Adrian released her as Brady pulled her into his arms. She gasped as her chest hit his chest, but he didn't notice as he inhaled against her neck and ran his hands over her body.

"Are you okay, mate? He didn't hurt you, did he?"

She shook her head. "I'm fine." She pressed her palms against him. He got the message and slowly stepped back but kept his hands on her waist. He stared down at the top of her dress and then reached up to fix the material just as she lowered her eyes. Her dress parted a little too far and more of her abundant breasts were showing.

He leaned forward and softly kissed her lips. She moaned.

He scrunched his eyes as Adrian pressed against her back. "You are hurt," Brady stated.

"My lips are sore from him kissing me. They'll heal. I think it's time to head home. I've had enough." She felt herself getting angry now. She didn't like feeling vulnerable, weak, and controllable. She didn't care for being outsmarted by a conniving wolf, and she realized how strong wolves were and how weak she was as a human.

"Sal, what is it?" Adrian asked her.

She shook her head. "Please. I just need to leave, to get out of here."

"Then we'll leave. I'll let the others know what happened. They'll get the car ready for us downstairs," Adrian said but then looked away from her a moment. He hadn't pulled out his cell phone or shown any indication of making a call. She found it peculiar as they headed inside, down another hallway to some elevator, and then out to the back parking lot. As they opened the door, all the men were there, including Reggie.

"Are you all right?" Reggie asked.

"Yes. Can you drive me home?" she asked.

"You're coming with us. Tonight could have been a lot worse. Get in the SUV now," Angus ordered as he joined them. He was so abrupt, and everyone reacted to his command, including her. She climbed into the backseat and tried to hide the pain she was in. She leaned back into the seat between Adrian and Brady. Delaney and Quinn sat across from them, and Angus and Eagan were in the front. Eagan was driving. She heard Angus making a phone call.

"Yes, I'm sure I smelled his scent, I just couldn't see where he was, but he was definitely there tonight, William," Angus stated into the phone. He spoke a little longer and she didn't know what it was all about.

She felt Adrian's hand move over her knee where her hands were and he clasped her hands. "You're safe now, Sal. You're with us and that's where you belong."

She released a sigh. She felt so tangled up in emotions. She was aroused by their masculinity and abilities. She felt scared after realizing that she wasn't invincible, but in fact vulnerable to becoming a victim at the hands of wolves. She couldn't help but wonder about these men's capabilities and the demands they could make or force upon her. She was angry for not being able to harm Jeremiah herself. She never met an obstacle or situation she couldn't overcome, defeat, or conquer. Until now. Until wolves.

* * * *

"What is she doing now?" Angus asked Quinn as they all stood in her town house while she grabbed some belongings. They decided that staying here at her place like sitting ducks wasn't safe. It angered him so much that Jaydin Carbarone flirted with her, Jett stared at her body, and Jeremiah trapped her on the balcony and kissed her. He didn't trust those men. He hated them and their pack. He needed to take precautions with their mate. Fennigan owned a lot of places, but they also had packs of family everywhere, including New York and New Jersey. He had another location, a private house thirty minutes outside of the city.

He was getting annoyed. "Go see what's taking her so damn long."

Eagan and Quinn went to ask her.

* * * *

Eagan pushed open the door and there stood Sal standing in only a pair of red thong panties and no bra. She was looking at something in the mirror when she spotted Quinn and Eagan. She covered herself with her arms best she could and disappeared behind the door to the bathroom. She came out pulling the robe against her body.

"What the hell? Are you going to try to force yourselves on me, too?" she snapped at them and Eagan didn't take his eyes off of her. His wolf was on edge. He could smell her fear and her upset, and he wanted to help her.

"We would never do that, Salina," Quinn whispered.

"Yeah right. Like I believe that for a minute. I saw what wolves are capable of in human form, remember? Just get out, please, and leave me alone." She turned away from them, holding the robe closed with her hand. She was shaking. Eagan could see it and sense it.

Eagan took her arm and turned her toward him gently. He placed his hand on her waist, causing the robe to come undone. He stared down into her eyes, also seeing her gorgeous, exposed breasts, but he focused on her. "You're shaking, you're scared, and tonight was upsetting for you. I understand that."

"We all do," Quinn added, stepping closer. She backed up, her legs hit the bed, and Eagan stepped closer.

"Upsetting for me? Try shocking, aggravating, and fucking unbelievable," she blurted out, her fists by her sides.

"Talk to us. We're not the enemy," Eagan whispered.

She shook her head and then took an unsteady breath. That was when he saw her breast and shoulder. It was black and blue.

"You're hurt?" he asked, pushing the robe off her shoulder and feeling his anger come to the surface. He locked his eyes on the discolored flesh. She squeezed her arms together, trying not to expose her breasts to their view, but he pulled her closer and now Quinn placed his hand against her bare back.

She gasped. "I'm fine."

"You're not fine," Quinn stated firmly.

"Please, just stop touching me. Just let me be alone to deal with this. It's too much and I...I'm feeling too many things at once. Please."

"She's hurt?" Adrian's thick, deep voice filled the bedroom and Sal turned toward him. Her face flushed, her eyes swept over their brother, and Eagan knew she felt the attraction to all of them. She was just scared and probably unsure of whether they could do her harm just as Jeremiah did.

"Let us take a look and determine the severity of this," Quinn said. He pressed against her back and wrapped his arm around her midsection, causing the robe to fall to her elbows.

"Damn, woman, you are a sight," Adrian said as he circled closer. Eagan knew the moment his eyes locked onto the injury.

"What the fuck happened? Did that piece of shit Carbarone wolf do that to you?" he asked, stepping closer.

Sal tried pulling the robe up higher, but Eagan reached up and cupped her cheek as Quinn inspected her shoulder.

"You're safe with us. All of us will protect you and help you to understand this relationship and bond we share. Just trust us and let go." He moved closer, needing to taste her lips, to kiss her and feel close to her to ensure she was indeed safe. He was right there when she closed her eyes, a sure sign of acceptance, and he covered her lips to take a taste of his mate.

Eagan explored her mouth and Sal reached up and pulled him to her.

Her hands squeezed against his upper arms to his shoulder and then his hair. She was so petite compared to them even though she was five feet seven.

She was standing barefoot, partially naked, and his wolf yearned to explore her body and mark her. He smoothed his hand along her hips under the robe and straight to her breast, full and round. She moaned into his mouth and pressed her body firmer against him. Behind them he could hear Adrian whispering to Sal.

"You're our woman, Sal. We need you. Let us love you, please."

Eagan took that moment to lift her up and against him. She straddled his waist, the robe fell to her hips, and she let her arms out of the sleeves to run her fingers through his hair and kiss him back. Their lips parted and she stared at him.

"This is insane. I can't believe how I feel. I must be losing my mind. I feel wild with need." She was panting, holding his gaze until Quinn reached over to trail a finger along her jaw.

"You're not losing your mind. You're gaining six men who will love you and cherish you always."

"Let us love you, lassie. Right here, right now, tonight, and you'll see that this is your destiny," Adrian told her.

Eagan couldn't stand it if she denied them her body, her heart, and her soul right now. His cock was hard and ready for her and it raced with desire.

"Let us in?" Eagan said.

He kissed her again and devoured her moans as he lowered her to the bed, one leg between her thighs.

When he released her lips, Sal lay there, hair flowing around her in curls of chocolate locks, her face was flushed, her breasts full and round, and he licked his lips.

"You have an exceptional body, baby."

He ran the palm of his hand up her body, from the top of her mound, over her breast and hardened, aroused nipple, to her throat. He cupped her face and leaned down to kiss her again on the lips.

"I need to taste you, make love to you, and claim you as mine."

She was panting, her chest heaving up and down, and she slowly lifted her torso up and down.

"Yes, do it. I want you, too. It's insane."

* * * *

Sal didn't know what had come over her. It seemed that every time these men were close by, her body was instantly horny for their cocks. They were so damn sexy and appealing, any damn woman wolf or human could see that. Their bodies were phenomenal, and their deep sexy voices penetrated to her core. But they were all so wild, untamed, and capable. They didn't fit in here in the United States, never mind New York. Their brogues, their attitudes, the size of them, and their amazing personalities energized the mood around them wherever they were. Being practically attacked by Jeremiah, a wolf and a man just like the Fennigan Pack, made her see how vulnerable she was. Did she need Fennigan Pack to really keep her safe? Was she defenseless without them? A lot of things were going through her head but most powerful were the attraction between her and these men. It took precedence over everything else.

She felt the bed dip and Adrian joined them on the left side. Quinn was now to the right of her.

They worked in sync. Eagan slowly pulled her panties down. His thick, hard thumbs and knuckles burned against her skin, and it was another indication that she was going through with this. She was going to have sex with these three men. Instantly she thought about Angus, Delaney, and Brady. Was Brady still upset about the situation? He hadn't said much to her on the way here.

All thought ceased the moment Adrian brushed his fingers along her jaw and stared into her eyes. "I've waited to taste you again. You're so sweet, angel." He leaned down and covered her mouth with his. At the same time Quinn cupped her breast and began to play with her nipple. She felt the tingling sensation as she tried to focus on Adrian's kissing. And then, as if she weren't overstimulated enough, Eagan licked against her pussy lips and she lost it. She pulled from Adrian's mouth and moaned as she thrust upward.

Eagan was slurping and sucking her clit, swallowing the cream she'd just released on a hell of a foreplay orgasm.

It shocked her, too, and Adrian seemed impressed.

"You're a fucking wild one, aren't you, lassie? You're going to love a cock in your pussy," he said, spreading her pussy lips and coating his fingers with her cream.

"Oh God." She moaned out.

"And how about one in this delicious mouth." Adrian trailed his fingers from her wet pussy lips to her mouth. He pressed his digits gently between her lips and she smelled her own scent. It was so damn erotic and she felt wild. She wanted to feel and act so experienced and sexy. She didn't want them to know how little she knew about sex, and even tasting her own cream off of his finger was a first for her. She licked his fingers, and he suckled her neck harder.

"Fuck yeah," Eagan whispered.

"Oh God." She spilled more cream, her body instantly reacting to their moans and words of pleasure.

"Then there's this sexy ass, so tight and firm," Eagan whispered, pressing a finger from her cunt to her puckered hole. Sal cried out another orgasm, and Adrian chuckled, his warm breath colliding against her sensitive skin.

She gasped at the thought, but then he kissed her again as he cupped her other breast and devoured her moans.

Below, Eagan pressed a finger to her cunt and began to thrust in and out of her pussy. She counterthrust against his fingers, feeling this internal, deep, strong itch that made her want to yell for these men to fuck her in every hole already. It was so damn outrageous, even her anus ached with need.

They pulled from her at once and Eagan lifted her thighs and brought her lower on the bed. He knelt down on the floor, placed her legs over his shoulders, and licked her from anus to pussy. She shivered.

Back and forth he stroked her privates with his tongue that seemed to be growing thicker and harder. He teased her in some wild, animalistic way that called to some deep inner goddess in her soul.

She nearly growled with need for more. She wiggled and panted, felt dizzy with need.

"Please, I need more. Please, Eagan." She thrust her pelvis up and down. She was oversensitive. Her ass even felt a tingling as it caressed against the soft fabric of the comforter. Even that aroused her cunt.

It was wicked crazy, and she knew as they explored further and eventually she had sex with them that things would never be the same again, and nor would she. She felt almost in a panic thinking that she would need to change first. Everything she did was in challenge against the norm. She never backed down, or ever gave up. She wouldn't start now.

"More," she chanted, feeling like she should assert some control here and not allow these Alpha men to have all the control and fun.

One glance toward the doorway and she saw the others. Angus had his arms crossed and looked concerned and angry as always. Delaney and Brady held her gaze, sniffed the air, and walked closer.

"Oh God," she moaned out and cried another release.

"She's ready for us," Adrian stated.

Eagan picked her up and kissed her on the mouth. She tasted her cream, felt aroused and needy like never before. He pulled back.

"You're ours tonight. All of ours." He turned her around, and there was Adrian. No kilt, no crisp dress shirt, just loads of muscles and one very thick, long, hard cock that was no way going to fit in her dormant pussy.

"Oh God, you're huge."

He smiled as he cupped her breast and thrust his hips upward. She felt the thick steel rod against her pussy and she closed her eyes and shivered.

"Take him inside of you, mate," Quinn ordered.

She lifted up, held Adrian's gaze, and something in her heart filled with acceptance. This was right. He was right for her.

Behind her Eagan used her cream to press against her anus. It felt wet and moist from his tongue already, but he was certain to explore her back there.

To the right there was Quinn, kneeling on the bed holding his long, thick cock in his hand and staring at her with hunger in his eyes.

"I want that mouth, woman." He reached up as Adrian pressed his cock upward between her wet pussy lips. She closed her eyes and moaned aloud, taking him into her body inch by inch.

"Oh God."

"Just relax those muscles and let him in," Eagan commanded as he pushed his finger between the tight rings of her ass, penetrating her.

"Oh God, it burns." She yelled out as another orgasm hit her from the simultaneous sensations.

"Sweet mother, you're so fucking tight, lassie. You're gripping my cock so damn hard. Fuck, I'm not gonna last," Adrian called out. He cupped her breasts and ran hard, thick thumbs along her nipples, making her shiver. It was sensation overload. Even the way his large hands felt cupping her breasts made her feel wild, feminine, and sexy.

"Bring that mouth here now, baby. We need to be inside you together at the same time. It will ensure the binding," Quinn said. She didn't really care what they wanted from her just as long as these sensations wouldn't stop. The itch grew stronger as she thrust her hips and began to ride Adrian.

"Fuck!" he roared again and then gripped her hips and thrust upward hard. She moaned and fell forward, only for Quinn to take her face between his hands and kiss her mouth. Adrian stroked her pussy as Quinn explored her mouth and then released her lips and lowered her head to his cock.

She knew what he wanted, and she obliged, licking the tip, then the base before pulling the bulbous head between her wet lips. Her nostrils flared. Something carnal and deep inside of her switched on, and she sucked him as deeply as she could into her mouth.

As she bobbed her head up and down, Adrian thrust his cock in and out of her. They were all moaning when she felt Eagan thrusting his fingers into her ass, causing this deep sensation to fill her to her core. She was almost there. Whatever it was, it would break her or cause some sort of amazing thing to happen, she just knew it.

Then Eagan pulled his fingers from her ass. She almost pulled away from Quinn to reprimand Eagan when she heard Eagan's voice and felt his hands caress her ass cheeks.

"Don't move. Don't worry, baby, I'm going to make you feel even better. Just relax and let me in."

She knew what he was going to do. A panicked feeling nearly caused her to tense up but then Adrian pumped his hips and cupped her breasts, pulling both nipples as she sucked on Quinn. A moment later she felt the bulbous top of Eagan's dick penetrate her anus and push right into her ass. It burned, she felt a "plop," and then she moaned against Quinn's cock.

"Fuck yeah. You're doing great, baby. Oh, I wish you could see this, Sal. Eagan's cock is deep in your ass. Fuck, you have a great ass." Quinn gave her ass cheek a slap.

She moaned and he cursed out as he held her head and pumped his hips a little faster.

She felt as if she might gag. He was pressing deeper, but then the sensations traveling over her body inside and out were so strong she gave in to the need for more and let go.

"That's it. Just like that. Let go and let us love you," Adrian told her. In and out they all fucked her in every hole. Over and over again her body orgasmed and released more cream. That sensation overcame her and she moaned against Quinn's cock as her body convulsed wildly. She felt like a broken dam as a sloshing sound echoed between them all. Quinn grabbed her tight.

"I'm there, baby. Here I come." He ejaculated into her mouth and she swallowed and tasted his bittersweet essence. He was musky, dark, and sensual. She loved the taste of him and felt so sexual and naughty. She couldn't believe she was having sex with three men. She never did any such thing before. Ever.

"Sal!" Eagan said her name and thrust two more times in her ass before exploding inside of her. He gripped her ass cheeks, pulled them and squeezed them, making her moan and hold on to Adrian. He was so big. Her legs could hardly straddle the man.

As Eagan pulled from her ass, she remembered the audience and locked gazes with Brady. He was undressed and so was Delaney.

Adrian took that moment to roll her across the bed to her back and let his body crush her a moment.

"Oh God." She moaned.

"Mine," Adrian said and lifted up and began to thrust into her fast and deep. She held on to his forearms. Her breasts swayed and bounced, and then he came, calling her name, filling her with his seed.

That was when she remembered they hadn't used protection. But she was on the pill.

She smiled down at Adrian, who cupped her cheek. "You're amazing, lassie. Absolutely amazing."

He kissed her, and when he lifted up, pulling away, Brady was there to take his place.

She looked at Brady's body.

He had a dusting of hair on his lower belly that led straight to his big cock. Her face felt flushed and he chuckled.

Running a fingertip along her own nipple, she shivered and tried to close her legs. But he was between them, his thick iron-hard thighs pressing against her inner thighs and making her pussy leak again. There had to be something seriously wrong with her. She was ready to have sex again. She should be achy.

But then came waves and waves of this sensation, a feeling deep inside her gut. It condoned what she was doing. A voice, a command made her accept this lovemaking and bonding for a reason. The more she accepted, the more these men touched her, caressed her, and expressed their desire, the lighter that darkness of shield seemed to get. She couldn't help but wonder if making love to these six men would reveal her true powers.

"You'll get used to it, baby. Having six mates to fill you up all the time will bring you such deep pleasure." Brady pinched her nipple. She gasped and he covered her mouth with his. He took from her hard and fast. His tongue explored her mouth while his hands explored her body. He caressed up her chest, cupping her breasts while using his thumbs to brush not so gently over her very sensitive nipples. She moaned and pushed her pelvis against him. Her pussy leaked, ready for cock.

He reached between them somehow and thrust a finger up into her cunt. She counterthrust, and then he pulled his fingers out, making her feel the loss only for him to replace them with his hard cock. He lifted her thighs, pulled from her mouth, and thrust into her hard.

She gripped his upper arms, the feel of steel arousing her further. "You're wild," she told him as she locked gazes with his green eyes.

"You don't know the half of it, mate." Brady thrust again and lifted her thighs high against him over his own thighs.

"Oh God, that feels so good. Keep going, faster, please, faster."

That itch and that need grew stronger. Brady pounded into her again and again until he found his release and growled deeply. She screamed aloud and then felt a pinch to her shoulder. Her head spun, her eyes rolled to the back of her head, and she thought she lost consciousness a moment. Then she felt Brady licking her shoulder. The others around them growled and joined them on the bed. She felt their hands caressing her body, and then Brady was panting against her shoulder.

"I was so worried about your safety. I can't lose another mate. I'll die protecting you. I promise, love. I promise." She felt his sincerity. She processed his words best she could in her clouded mind.

He felt responsible for their last mate's death. They each did. She read that in their thoughts and felt so sad for them.

Brady lifted up after he squeezed her and then Delaney was there.

He picked her up and kissed her deeply on the mouth. She ran her fingers through shoulder-length dark-brown hair and inhaled his scent. Her body, though achy now, released more cream and indicated she was ready for more. He pressed her against the wall and continued to kiss her. She reached under them, feeling carnal and brazen, and aligned his cock with her pussy.

"Are you sure you're not too achy?" he asked, kissing along her neck and then to her shoulder where Brady had bitten her. It was so odd, and she should be freaking out right now, but instead she felt relief. It felt right.

"I'm positive. I need you, too." She leaned forward and kissed him as she lifted up and then lowered onto his thick, hard shaft.

She felt Delaney's hands smooth over her ass and underneath her. As he thrust his hips, stroking his cock into her wet cunt, she felt the cream drip down her ass and she wanted more.

She tilted her head back, pulling from his lips, and she saw Angus. He stared at her, and his brothers stared at him. Something was going on between them.

She moaned and held Angus's gaze as Delaney thrust into her again and again.

* * * *

"She wants you, Angus. She fucking wants all of us. We need to mate with her to protect her," Adrian stated to Angus, but Angus feared losing another mate. What if he lost Sal, too?

"You can't ponder over the past. That was out of our control. We never had the chance to bind with Margo like we're doing here with Sal. She wants us and needs us. We can't do this without you," Quinn added.

"You're our Alpha. She needs you and she needs all of us. Take her. Bite into her shoulder and mark her so that the Carbarone stay clear of our mate," Brady stated.

"Angus, now. She's ready for you now," Delaney stated.

Angus felt his wolf growing antsy and protective. He wanted to make love to Sal and to mark her to protect her like he and his brothers never had done before. The need and desire was so great, yet he was fearful. Never in his life had he ever been so fearful except when he failed Margo and wasn't certain if he should live or die.

"She needs you now," Quinn said aloud.

Gods, direct me now. Please don't let us lose Sal. Help us to protect her always.

Angus pulled off his shirt just as Delaney pulled Sal from the wall and brought her over to the bed. He turned around and sat down then lowered onto his back. She took over, making love to him on top, and Angus stared at her body.

He reached out slowly, almost afraid to touch her and make that physical contact because there would be no turning back. He didn't want to fuck up again and cost Sal her life. Could he be the man, the Alpha mate she needed, and the leader to his brothers they deserved and expected?

His fingers touched her ass and back, and that was it. He closed his eyes and caressed her back and shoulders, feeling her soft, silky skin.

"Yes." She moaned and thrust her ass back at him.

"Fuck." Delaney roared his release, and she screamed hers.

"You're beautiful," Delaney told her.

She leaned down and kissed him, and then Angus wrapped an arm around her waist and hoisted her up. Delaney got out of the way and Angus placed her on all fours. He kissed her shoulder where the bruise was. Her scent, the taste of her skin, and the smell of his brothers' scents filled his nostrils.

"Is it very sore?" he asked about the bruise. She shook her head.

He smoothed one palm along her belly to her breast. She was well endowed. He cupped the delicate flesh and licked against her skin right over his brother's mark.

"I want you."

"Yes," she replied without hesitation.

She was on all fours as he maneuvered his cock behind her. Her ass stuck out toward him. Her pussy glistened with cream as it dripped between her thighs. She had an amazing body, muscular, firm, yet curved in all the right places. He used his hands to glide down her flesh, his wolf growing more and more impatient to sink his cock deep within her.

He lowered down, caressing her body and her luscious curves along the way. He licked her pussy from behind, and her cream covered his tongue. His wolf growled low.

"Isn't she fucking delicious?" Eagan stated.

"Yes."

She shivered from his warm breath colliding with her sensitive pussy.

"You are perfect. Perfect for six big Alpha wolves." He aligned his cock with her pussy. He massaged her ass, spreading her cheeks and zeroing in on her anus. She didn't seem to realize how much of a submissive position she was in. It meant so much to take her this way, from behind with access to her ass and her cunt, as he thrust his cock as deep as she could take him.

Slowly as not to hurt her, and to force his wolf and the man to take their time, he pressed inside of her.

Sal moaned and gripped the comforter.

"Easy, mate, you took my brothers. You can handle me, too." He knew his tone sounded pompous and commanding. That was Angus and Sal needed to accept him this way. He ran his palm back and forth over her back, and she felt so feminine and lovely to him. His heart ached with the realization that he was already far too connected even before sinking his cock into her.

He ran his hands along her hips and her ribs. As he reached underneath her and cupped her breasts, keeping his cock only half in her cunt, the little minx pushed back, trying to get him to go deeper.

"Easy, mate. When I'm ready."

She mumbled something. He leaned forward and nipped her shoulder, making her gasp and lower slightly. Then he thrust into her pussy balls-deep from behind.

He held himself within her as she moaned and shook. Taking his time as he tried to control his own heavy breathing, he began a series of deep, slow thrusts. He stroked her cunt, feeling her inner muscles grip his shaft and make him moan in agony. He needed so much from her, and she creamed again, lubricating his movements.

"I can't go slow."

"Then don't," she told him. "Take me, Angus. Make me yours, too."

That was it. Angus pulled back and then thrust into her again and again. He was moving so fast, so deeply that Sal cried out another orgasm as she fell to her chest. He gripped her hips and thrust again and again, her ass in the air, her neck and shoulder exposed. He felt his wolf surface as he exploded inside of her. He leaned down, still pumping his hips, and he bit her, sealing their fate, and allowing the desire and bond to begin.

Please, by the gods and goddesses, keep her safe. Please.

Chapter 10

"You're being awfully quiet, Torque. What's going on that you're not sharing with us?" Vargon asked.

Torque was in a dead stare at Jeremiah. "You shouldn't have touched her."

"She is to be mine, and my brothers'. She most definitely will not belong to Fennigan Pack. Fuck those mutts and their entire bloodline of royal bullshit."

"Jeremiah, that confrontational attitude is what nearly cost you your life last night," Torque sated.

Jeremiah's eyes widened as he stood up and gave Torque his wolf eyes. "My life? No, more like their lives. I could have easily taken Brady."

"Not a chance, and Adrian was there, too. Those two are the craziest of the fucking bunch. They have quadruple the number of kills you do, so I'd say you were given a second chance at life."

"Fuck you."

"Enough! Sit down, Jeremiah. You indeed may have cost us the opportunity we needed to persuade the little magic woman to our side. Torque, tell me what you found out. Where do we go from here?"

Torque looked at Vargon. "You are right, your opportunity may be lost. If Fennigan Pack know what Sal is, if she confided in them or perhaps they were told by someone in their extended family, then the opportunity could be lost."

"Never," Jeremiah called out.

Vargon gave his nephew another warning look. "By extended family, do you mean Dani and Declan Pack?"

Jeremiah growled low.

"Indeed. Dani is a healer. She also contains the blood of a vampire besides a wolf. If the Fennigan Pack are mates to Sal, then it's over."

"Whoa! Mates? Where the hell did that come from? My brothers and I are her mates. We staked a claim first. She was untouched, unmarked by them. This is not allowed." Jeremiah paced the room.

"Jeremiah, it doesn't matter. Whomever she gives her body to and accepts the claiming from, they become her mates. I did sense a good amount of Fennigan Pack on her. It could have already happened."

"Then why was she there without them last night? Why wasn't she marked accordingly? No, I saw how her eyes absorbed my body. She was interested in me, Jaydin, and Jett. She will be ours, even if I have to kill Fennigan Pack."

"Jeremiah, that is not the way the law works. The Circle will find you guilty and summon you to your death. Then you will have nothing, especially not Sal," Torque told him.

"Then figure something out so my brothers and I can have her. Otherwise, if I can't have her, then no one can, especially not Brady Fennigan and the rest of his pack."

* * * *

Sal felt so exhausted she couldn't move. She actually didn't want to because the warmth that encased her body was so delightful. She never slept this heavy. She moved and felt the ache in her shoulder.

"Ouch," she said, her voice deep and sexy. It didn't even sound like her. She blinked her eyes open just as she heard the growls. The bed was big, at least king size and covered with white fluffy pillows and a comforter. She looked straight ahead as she eased her body up, and locked gazes with three dark black wolves. At first she thought they were three of the six brothers, but then the one in the center snarled, baring its sharp teeth as it drooled and slowly moved closer.

Every ounce of her knew that it wasn't being friendly. Her gut instinct was to run, and as she eased the covers back, she felt the wolf's hot breath and heard the deep growl. She gasped. Her heart felt as if it were in her throat as she turned to the left and there was another wolf right next to the bed. She tried to calm her breathing. She felt as if she weren't really here, couldn't be here in a situation like this.

Then came the tingling sensation as she stared at the wolf. His eyes glowed yellow and black. She saw him transform before her eyes. The moment she saw Jaydin she screamed out in terror and then came his bite, ending her life.

"Salina! Salina, you're okay."

"Jaydin?" she whispered.

Delaney scrunched his eyes together and growled low.

She gasped and locked gazes with Delaney. She felt the hands on her thigh and the other on her shoulder from the other side. She turned quickly, still on edge from her dream, and took in the sight of Eagan. His ocean-blue eyes were filled with great concern for her. He caressed her body. She tried to swallowed and look around the room. She didn't see the wolves. She didn't see Jeremiah or Jaydin.

"I saw the wolves. He bit me. I—"

She raised her hand to run her fingers through her hair and the pain struck her shoulder. She also realized she was naked and in bed with Eagan and Delaney.

"Salina, it was a bad dream. You're safe here with us. They can't harm you. Do you understand?" Eagan asked.

She nodded her head but tried to process her thoughts and her surroundings while using her other hand to pull the sheets up against her bare chest.

She glanced toward the doorway. There was no one there. She looked at the bed, the comforter, and pillows. They were nearly identical to the ones in her dream. If that was what it was, a dream.

"You're shaking, baby," Delaney whispered as he caressed her arm while Eagan told her to lay back down and rest.

"It's early, Salina. You're okay. It was just a bad dream." She lowered down into the softness and warmth of the pillows between Eagan and Delaney. She stared up at the ceiling a moment, her breathing calmer and her mind whirling in numerous directions.

"Can you control your anger when you're both in wolf form?" she asked them. Both men leaned up on their elbows facing her. Delaney caressed her belly over the sheet, while Eagan reached up and placed his fingers under her chin.

"Of course we can. Our wolf is just as important and equally powerful as the man."

She stared into Eagan's blue eyes and she could sense his strong spirit. She felt at ease despite her line of questioning.

"Are you certain, Eagan? I mean, if there was anything that could make you lose all control and just kill, what would it be?" she asked.

He looked at Delaney and she saw them exchange a look before they stared down at her.

"If someone hurt our mate, we would kill them," Eagan stated.

"Do you know who it was?" she asked.

"You're our mate now. The past is over. We focus on the future. Our future," Delaney stated firmly. She glanced at him. Delaney and his shoulder-length hair appeared wild. He was a force to reckon with just as Angus and all the brothers were. But to her, Delaney seemed most quiet about it. Was it strategic habit or just his true self?

"How can you move ahead in life if you don't remember where you've been?" she asked.

Eagan caressed her cheek and then leaned down and kissed the corner of her mouth. "It seems we've been given a second chance in life. A chance at having love, and truly bonding with our mate. That's all that matters to us now. Serving you, caring for you, and providing for you are our present and our future," he told her. He covered her mouth and kissed her deeply. She ran her fingers through his hair and absorbed his scent, his powerful personality, and then she hugged him close. She tried to move and felt the ache, not only in her shoulder but between her legs.

"You're sore, aren't you?" Delaney asked as Eagan released her lips and moved the sheet down to check on the large bruise.

"Just a little." She replied. But truth was she felt really sore. Everywhere. She hadn't had sex in a couple of years. She never had anal sex, and she certainly never allowed three men to take her together, and then three more after that.

She felt her cheeks warm. Delaney caressed her with the back of his hand.

"What's that blush about?" he asked.

"Just trying to figure out what was real and what was fantasy. I feel like I've been stuck in a dream and any moment I'm going to wake up in my bed at home and feel like an idiot."

"Not going to happen. It's real, Salina. Our lovemaking, you calling out our names when we were deep inside of you. I can help you remember if you've forgotten already," Eagan teased as he gently stroked her nipple then nuzzled against her neck.

She giggled and then gave him a nudge.

Delaney caressed his arm over her waist and pulled her tighter against him to snuggle.

"Close your eyes and rest. When the others get back, we'll make something to eat and plan the next step."

"The next step to what, Delaney?" she asked.

"To our future. Things need to change. We need to protect you."

* * * *

"Are you prepared for her to fight you on leaving New York, never mind the country?" Dani asked Angus over the phone.

"Ireland is our home. It's where most of our pack is. I think it's best for her to get used to her new place as our mate."

"But Angus, from how you described her, from her professional position in law enforcement, I don't think she'll be too keen on being dragged halfway around the world because you demand it."

"I just don't want to take any chances. She's a risk taker, and very aggressive. She thinks that she can handle any given situation, and last night, well, last night was a close call. Brady and Adrian are upset. Brady was going to take on Jeremiah Carbarone right there. I don't like that Jeremiah is interested in Sal. His brothers were even sniffing around."

"I understand your concern. Believe me, I'd like nothing more than to see the entire Carbarone family destroyed, but there are rules. You all need to mark her, and send the message that she is yours."

"We're working on it, but this isn't easy, Dani. I still can't believe that she's our mate. That the gods have granted us another chance."

"Angus, you all deserve another chance. You deserve happiness. Margo cared for you all so deeply, but she risked her life to save others. The great battle of the Goddesses of the Circle against that evil demon made all our packs sustain heavy losses. But it is our destiny to keep the peace, to counter any attempts at ignoring our kind's rules and laws. That's your job and your brothers' jobs. You've focused on everyone else but yourselves for quite some time. Enjoy this process with your mate. Make her feel comfortable in learning about each of you, and I'm certain she will submit. Besides, the case she was working on with Reggie has gained the attention of the Brothers of Were and Special Crimes Unit 6."

"Special Crimes Unit 6? Is this because of Torque still being alive? They're one of the few teams that hunt rogue Magi, wizards, and other rogue species."

"Yes, it seems after you notified William Declan and gave him the heads-up about the case, he and his brothers were contacted by Unit 6. They didn't give many details but asked Declan Pack and Reggie to stand down."

"Shit, that sounds pretty damn serious. Now I am really concerned."

"Angus, focus on getting your mate to submit and seal the bond. I'm a certain she will adjust accordingly."

"Just as you so eagerly submitted to your mates?" he asked.

She chuckled. "What is that saying? Oh yes, if I knew then what I know now."

He laughed.

"I'm sure that learning about all these mystical creatures existing and walking the earth side by side with the humans has been a shock in itself for her. Hell, I nearly passed out the moment I saw firsthand that vampires exist."

"Yeah, there is a lot for her to learn. But I also fear the scent she emits. It's so very appealing, yet I sensed a wall of some sort, even in intimacy."

"As we both know, the gods and goddesses decide when it is right to reveal one's true self. With time it will happen, and since your enemies, our enemies, have taken an interest, I would guard her completely."

"Thanks, Dani. I'll let you know when we'll be flying out. I have a call in to Ava and William. They would like us to stay at the castle in Ireland when we return. Ava is very interested in meeting Salina."

"Very good. But remember what I said. She needs reassurance despite her tough, capable attitude. It's all new and scary."

"I will. Talk to you soon."

Angus hung up the phone and leaned back in his chair. They had brought Salina to their estate in New Jersey right outside of the city. She had been exhausted last night and even now, nearly noontime, she still slept with Eagan and Delaney. He closed his eyes, thinking about what Eagan had told him through their mind link as she woke up having a nightmare. His phone rang, interrupting his thoughts. He glanced at the caller ID and saw that it was Reggie.

"Hey, cousin, what's going on?"

"Well, a lot actually. I'm assuming that Sal is with you guys since she was a no-show at work."

"Yep, still sleeping."

"That's great. Except I think we may have a situation on our hands."

Angus sat forward as Adrian and Brady entered the room. He placed the call on speaker. "Go ahead. Brady and Quinn are here, too."

"I got into work this morning and our lieutenant was asking me all these questions about Sal. Who she was with last night? What happened between her and Carbarone? He also asked why my cousins were in town and being so protective of Sal. Anyway, I had the feeling that I should probably not mention the fact that you are mates, considering that as we were talking, the lieutenant's secretary said that Jaydin Carbarone was on the line."

"Jaydin? Why is Benjamin talking to Jaydin?"

"Exactly my question. I decided that this was more than just coincidence, so when the lieutenant headed out about an hour ago for lunch, I followed him. He went into Vargon Carbarone's apartment building."

"Shit, do you think he's working for Carbarone?" Brady asked.

"I sure as shit wouldn't put it past him. You guys should know that Benjamin has had a thing for Sal for quite some time. He's been pushy lately from my perspective. Sal has ignored his advances, but still, I don't trust Benjamin, and after the incident with Jeremiah last night, I'd say keep your mate close."

"That fucker better stay clear of our woman," Quinn stated.

"He can't come near her if she's in Ireland on our land and in our pack territory," Angus said firmly.

"Ireland? You're taking her to Ireland?" Reggie asked.

"We discussed it early this morning," Brady said and looked at Angus. He held his brother's gaze. Brady was still pissed off and worried about Jeremiah's interest in Salina.

"What did Sal say about this?" Reggie asked.

"We haven't discussed it with her fully, but I'm certain our mate will submit to our command," Angus said.

"Submit to your command? What the fuck, Angus? She's not a wolf. She's not going to go so easily. You really don't understand what kind of woman she is."

"I certainly do. She's stubborn, set in her ways, and passionate about her career. She can make the changes necessary in order to be our mate."

"Holy shit. You are in for it. Listen, do what you think is right, but don't push her too far, she'll fight you tooth and nail. She may even leave your ass."

"That's not going to happen. She'll submit," Brady added.

"Reggie, you worry about investigating the lieutenant. Perhaps Carbarone and his pack are up to no good. If the lieutenant is involved, maybe others in the department are as well. We'll need to weed through the trash and clean house. Make sure you talk with Task Force Eight, the Lawkins Pack. Let Blaise know what's going on, and they can assist in the investigation. I trust them entirely," Angus said.

"As do I. They're a very strict, powerful force the Goddess of the Circle, Kamea, appointed as head of law enforcement in New York City. They'll find the rats. In fact, the Lawkins brothers take their jobs very seriously and they know a lot of people. I'll get on it. Good luck with Sal. Talk to you soon."

Angus disconnected the call and looked at Brady and Quinn.

"We need to keep her safe. If it pisses her off, so be it."

"Agreed," Quinn stated.

"Agreed," Brady added.

Angus felt his gut clench. Salina was definitely going to fight them on this, but as much as he respected her profession, her passion for her job, and her tough, independent attitude, she wasn't prepared to fight against wolves. Jeremiah had caught her off guard and unprotected. That couldn't ever happen again.

Chapter 11

"McCarthy, it's just a bit of a friendly warning. There's no need to freak out," Investigator Jimmy Lannigan told McCarthy Skylar over the phone.

"Don't freak out? How the hell can you ask me to not freak out when you tell me something like this? How long has Vargon Carbarone been infiltrating my pack?" he asked, his Irish brogue deepening the angrier he got. Jimmy could picture the redheaded Alpha with his deep blue eyes and firm, muscular jaw. He and his brothers were a tough crew of Alphas, but they were holding on to a small pack slowly dying out with the lack of females to produce more male pups.

"I don't have proof of them infiltrating your packs and territory as of yet. Zespian along with Fagan Pack are working on that as we speak. We haven't exactly taken our eyes off of them since all the trouble they started during the inauguration of the goddesses to their positions above the Circle."

"How about Fennigan Pack? Where the hell are they? Those crazy bastards have been waiting for the opportunity to crush Carbarone. He had a hand in their mate's death. The whole lot of them should have been punished by the new Circle."

"I hear your frustration and Fennigan Pack is dealing with this issue from where they are in America."

"America? What the fuck are they doing in America?" McCarthy asked.

"They've been keeping a close eye on Carbarone and his men. I just called so that you were aware of the situation so you can plan accordingly. I'd be careful who you trust with any plans, McCarthy."

"I get it. I'm pretty pissed off. No fucking New York asshole pack of troublemakers is going to come over here and take my land, my pack, right from underneath me."

"He could follow tradition and challenge you for it."

McCarthy was silent a moment. "Then so be it."

* * * *

"I'm fine, Quinn, stop fussing over my damn shoulder." Sal snapped at Quinn again as she tried unsuccessfully to pull the sheet from the bed so her body was covered before she walked across the bedroom.

"I'd watch that tongue there, lassie, or you'll be getting some swats on that sexy round ass of yours," Adrian told her as he eyed her body over. That damn man was so forceful, but throw in the accent, and shit, her pussy clenched with desire and her body shivered in anticipation of being placed over his thighs. The man had a set of thick, tree-trunk thighs on him that reminded her of when they made love so forcefully.

"Like that is going to happen," she countered, then pulled the sheet and nearly fell over. Quinn was there to scoop her up into his arms and carry her to the bathroom. He stared at her face as she started to speak as if to reprimand him.

"Close it," he said firmly. Now his brogue was all deep and sexy. His muscular chest and neck were eye level with her. She looked into his eyes and damn did she get all warm and aroused again. These men were walking fantasies. She needed to gain some control here. They were treating her like she could break.

"I can walk, damn it. I don't need you carrying me around like some damsel in distress. What the hell?" She raised her voice and

Quinn flipped her quickly, making her head spin, and she had to grab onto him as she squealed, thinking he might drop her. His large hands were on her hips, her breasts bounced from the abrupt movement, and she felt Quinn's thick cock press against her belly.

"You listen here and listen good. You're our mate, and we'll carry you, kiss you, and pleasure you whenever we damn well please. This stubborn, independent attitude needs to end now."

She tried calming her breathing but something inside her seemed to be more powerful than the need to tell Quinn off. Her nipples tingled. How the hell could that happen when he wasn't even touching her?

He stared deeply into her eyes and she held his gaze. The flow of calm and love encompassed her body. She eased her grip and then closed her eyes, trying to figure out where this was coming from.

She felt his lips against her cheek and ear. "You're my mate and I adore you. You're so sexy, smart, and tough, but I won't tolerate being ignored or pushed away by my mate. By the woman my wolf and the man in me needs so very close."

He kissed along her neck and she pressed against him. His palm caressing down her hip over her thigh and then between her legs heightened her arousal. She felt her pussy cream right before his fingers bushed across her pussy lips.

"So wet and sweet for me. You know it feels good, it feels right. My touch, my scent will always do this to you. You're meant for me and for my brothers. You're fucking lovely, mate." He kissed her chin and then made his way to her lips. When he spoke so seductively against them and pressed his fingers up into her, she gasped.

"Open for me, mate. Let me get your pussy ready for my cock. I need to be inside of you." He kissed her again and again, and as she parted her thighs, he pressed fingers deeper and began to stroke her pussy.

"Oh, Quinn." She moaned aloud and he pulled her bottom lip between his teeth, giving it a tug.

"Fucking wet and ready, just like I love it." He pulled his fingers from her cunt and lifted her up and against him. He pushed his boxers down and aligned his cock with her pussy.

He held her as if she weighed nothing at all. There was no wall to lean against and he pushed her hips down as her pussy took in his thick cock. She was amazed at his strength, his agility, and all his beautiful muscles. Her pussy ached as she moaned and closed her eyes. But she still wanted him, and something carnal and wild came over her. She spread her palms up his chest and pinched both nipples.

"Fuck, lassie, you drive me wild."

He walked closer to the counter, pressed her ass on the towel on the edge, and plowed into her. In and out he pumped his hips and she caressed her hands over his muscles. The dips, the ridges, and the feel of iron underneath her delicate hands made her incredibly aroused.

"God, you're gorgeous, and so big and strong. I can't explain these feelings. I need so much," she admitted to him.

He pulled back and thrust into her again, making her lose her breath.

"I can't fucking take it. I can't take the feel of your delicate hands on me, the scent of your arousal, and the magnificent aroma of your scent."

He pulled out and thrust back into her over and over again.

"And your words, your voice, everything about you makes my wolf and my man wild and needy. Fuck!" he blurted out and kissed her deeply. He plunged his tongue into her mouth in sync with his strokes. She gripped onto him and tried to counterthrust but his hold and his speed was so unbelievably wild she lost it and orgasmed, screaming his name.

"Salina, oh by the gods, Salina!"

He thrust three more times then came inside of her. His eyes glowed as he leaned forward and bit into her shoulder. Salina cried out and then gripped him against her, hugging him so tight as both their bodies convulsed together.

He held her just like that for minutes as they tried to calm their breathing. He pulled back, their bodies sticking to one another, and he grabbed her face between his hands.

"Bound for eternity. You are mine and I am yours. I will protect you with my life, Salina. With my life." When he kissed her, she closed her eyes, overwhelmed with her own deep feelings for Quinn.

* * * *

"What was that call all about?" Eagan asked Angus as he, Brady, and Delaney stood in the office.

"It was William. I had him check into something for me," Angus replied, running his fingers through his hair. He was greatly concerned.

"Well, tell us. You've been blocking your thoughts most of the morning, Angus. It must be serious," Brady stated firmly. He thought of his brothers as his equal, but he also knew they saw him as their Alpha and leader to their pack. Any of them could serve the same position.

He looked at them.

"At the dedication party, while you all were watching over Sal, and you, Brady, had the confrontation with Jeremiah, I was walking through the area and had noticed a man standing beside Jaydin and Vargon. Something drew me to him so I got a closer look and when I came near I realized who it was. Brady, you were telling us through our link about the danger Sal was in and how you and Adrian were there. I lost my focus for a moment and the next thing I know, the man was gone."

"So who was he?" Delaney asked.

"I wasn't certain at first. I mean, my wolf swore it was Torque, the wizard, but then something came over my mind. It blocked the thought, put it out of my head, until after I made love with Salina."

"I thought he died when Margo did?" Brady asked, sounding perturbed.

"We all did. He had disappeared and no one knew where he was and assumed he died in that battle. So many lives were lost that day," Eagan added.

"I'm not liking this feeling I have. It doesn't sit right with me. I called Vanderlan. He knew Torque, and had concerns over his loyalty to the Circle," Angus stated.

"What did he think?" Eagan asked.

"He was concerned immediately. He said he would look into it with his resources. Let's think about this. Torque was there, in disguise and standing with Vargon Carbarone. Why? The Carbarone Pack is already on the watch list."

"You're thinking guilty by association?" Brady asked.

"You're damn straight," Angus replied.

"They were talking to Salina," Delaney whispered then ran his fingers through his hair and looked up toward the ceiling as if thinking of Salina upstairs with the others.

"She was?" Angus asked. Then he rubbed his chin. "How come I don't remember seeing them with her? Fuck." He walked toward the window.

"There was a lot going on. We were all trying our hardest to watch her but keep a distance. People were probably in the way," Eagan stated.

"No. No, it's more than that. This is what concerns me about protecting her. I can't. I'll fail her like I failed Margo," Angus stated.

"Fuck that, you did not fail Margo. None of us did. She went in there on her own and alerted us when she was already at the location. If we had known then, we would have accompanied her. We all would have helped plan her protection. You're reading into this, Angus," Brady stated.

"No, I'm obviously weak. Torque must have used something on me to block me from noticing him and believing it was him. He could have grabbed Salina. What if he wants her? What if he knows what that special scent she has means?"

"Calm down and be rational," Delaney stated. "If Torque did such a thing, it disappeared when you made love to Salina. Perhaps our bond with her, the fact that she is now our mate, has something to do with all of it. We need advice and guidance. Taking her back to Ireland, to our pack, to the family is the best thing we can do right now for all of us."

"Yes, Angus, it will strengthen our bond with Salina. It will empower our minds and our spirits and destroy the weaknesses from our pasts. We need to take her there, it's best for all of us," Brady said.

"Then we do it. But I still think one of you may need to take over as Alpha."

"No," Brady, Eagan, and Delaney stated together.

"It's not up for discussion now. Let's take care of our mate and then a decision will be made. Marking her is imperative."

* * * *

Adrian pulled Salina into his arms and wrapped her in a towel the moment she emerged from the shower with Quinn.

He kissed her forehead, and she laid her cheek against his chest.

"This is so wild. I've never felt anything like this before. I almost feel like I'm having some out-of-body experience," she whispered.

Adrian caressed her hair and then he undid the towel to help her dry off. He stared at her abundant breasts and leaned down to take a taste. "You're beautiful, and this is real." He licked across the nipple and she shivered.

"I need you, lassie." He lifted her up into his arms. She straddled his waist and kissed him on the mouth. He walked her toward the bedroom and then pressed her down onto the bed. She pulled from his lips, and her brown eyes twinkled with desire.

He ran the palms of his hands up her thighs, spreading them. She covered his hands, following their direction, and lifted her torso up and down. He could see her cream glistening from her cunt and he closed his eyes and inhaled. His wolf stirred with desire. He would make love to her, bite her, and leave his mark. The bond was growing stronger.

"Talk to me, Adrian. I love the sound of your brogue and that deep, hard voice of yours. It does something to me."

He opened his eyes and smiled down at her. He squeezed her hips. "This body does something to me, Salina."

She smiled. "Like what?"

He used his thumbs to press against her pussy lips as he leaned forward and licked another nipple.

"Mmmm. That feels nice," she told him.

He pulled on the hardened bud then swirled his tongue over it. "Do ya know what your little moans do to me, lassie?"

She shook her head.

"They make me want to fuck and claim you. Every fucking inch of you." He used his finger to stroke from her pussy to her anus.

"Oh God, Adrian, I can't take it. Please, do it. Please."

He lowered down, kissing her skin and licking a pathway to her belly button and then to her mound.

When he licked over her pussy, she moaned again. Then he lifted her thighs and licked over her anus.

"Do it, please. I can't take it."

He saw cream drip from her cunt, and he pressed his face to her pussy and inhaled. She gripped his hair.

"Adrian, damn it."

He chuckled, knowing his warm breath stimulated her even more. "What is it, lassie? I'm kind of busy right now."

He locked gazes with her as he licked her pussy lips, his eyes staring up over her taut belly. She widened her thighs to hold his gaze.

"Fuck me, Adrian. I want you, too. Now."

He chuckled deeply and squeezed her thighs wider. She gasped. "You'll be learning mighty quickly, mate, that your men are the bosses in bed."

Her eyes glazed over and then a fire brewed within them. "Maybe it's you who will be learning, laddie, that this here woman doesn't take a liking to orders."

Her challenge hardened his dick and aroused his wolf. He squinted at her. "You sure you want to challenge me, mate?"

"Did I stutter?" she asked, very seriously, but he saw the smile in her eyes.

She was pushing him on purpose and it was time to set her straight. "Lesson number one, I am your Alpha and disobeying me in any fashion will cost you punishment."

"Punishment?" she asked in shock, and in a flash he lifted her up, turned her onto her belly over his lap, and smacked her on the ass.

"Adrian!" she squealed and he chuckled, the sight of her round ass and her trying to sit up while she pushed the abundant curls from her face was a sight.

"You shall obey your Alpha. Say it," he demanded as he caressed her ass and she wiggled to get free. But it was no use, he was stronger and she was in an awkward position.

"What the hell did she do?" Quinn asked.

"She challenged me. She needs to learn that we are her Alphas and we have the final say."

Quinn walked over and bent down. He pushed the strands of hair from her face and looked at her.

"You don't want to mess around with Adrian. He's the disciplinarian of the group when it comes to the bedroom."

"I will not be ordered around. He just spanked me," she stated, sounding absolutely shocked.

"Good. You deserve more. Continue on, Adrian. Our mate needs to learn she's the mate to Alphas." Quinn smiled then kissed her on the mouth. He stood up and Salina growled.

"This is insane. Oh." She moaned and Adrian pressed a finger between thighs to her wet cunt. He moved the cream back and forth over her pussy and then to her anus.

"Adrian, please."

"Who is in charge and who is here to protect you?" he asked as he continued to explore her pussy and ass with his fingers.

"Adrian!" she reprimanded.

He thrust a thick digit up into her cunt and she moaned aloud. In and out he stroked, and then she wiggled and moaned.

"Who is in charge of you, your safety, and this body?"

She didn't answer, so he pulled his finger from her cunt and gave her ass a spank. He caressed his palm over the pink cheek and then smacked the other cheek. She moaned and wiggled.

"Who?" he asked again and she exhaled.

"Oh God, I can't believe I'm turned on by this. Oh God, I've lost my mind. This is it."

He smacked her ass two more times and then caressed away the sting before he pressed a finger to her pussy.

"Who, mate?" he asked.

"You, Goddamn it, you and my other five control-freak Alphas."

He had to hide his chuckle. He lifted her up, placed her on the bed on all fours, and pressed against her as he held her wrists. Her palms were down and her head up as she moaned from the sensations.

"That's right, mate, your Alphas." He licked against her shoulder and neck where his brothers' marks now sat. They were a sign of their binding and hopefully a deterrent to any other man or wolf who was interested in their mate.

He used his thick, hard thighs to press hers further apart.

She tightened up and moaned, slowly coming some more just from the feel of him.

"Your body knows, mate. It knows to succumb to my wolf, that its Alpha wants in."

"Yes, Oh God, Adrian, I feel it. I need you."

He smiled and then reached back and aligned his cock with her pussy from behind.

"You're mine, always." He pressed into her slowly, but as her vaginal muscles clung to his cock, he lost the control to go slow. The sight of her back, her ass, and toned shoulders was such a turn-on. Their mate was strong, gorgeous, and resourceful. He thrust into her to the hilt and she moaned and thrust back. Adrian wrapped an arm around her midsection and whispered against her ear.

"Hold on, lassie, you're about to get fucked really good."

He pulled out and thrust back in as he scraped his teeth across her skin. Salina moaned again and shook from her first orgasm, lubricating his thick, steel-hard shaft.

"Fuck, baby, I love the little moans and groans you make. If spanking makes you this turned on, I can't wait to see what you do when I tie you down and have my way with you."

"Oh God, Adrian. You're so wild." She gasped as he continued to stroke into her harder, faster.

The sight of his brothers' marks, her sexy body, and his wolf's need to claim and mark her was overwhelming. He felt his eyes change and his incisors extend. The thrusts were so deep and wild they were making the bed rock. He was trying to hold off but it was all too much for him. Even the sound of his balls slapping against her ass and wet pussy aroused his wolf, along with her scent, delicious and all consuming. He thrust again and Salina screamed her release as he exploded inside of her. He leaned forward then felt his wolf's hunger and need to mark and claim Salina take over all thoughts. He bit into her shoulder as he closed his eyes, and he saw her true self.

The magic within her sparkled and he sensed for that moment the powerful ability she had, and the barrier that was in place weakened with every mark from her mates. Although he couldn't tell what her ability was, he knew she was pure and good. And then her face appeared with a weak smile of uncertainty, and he heard her voice.

"Are you really here in my mind and heart, Adrian?"

"Holy shit, yes. Yes, I see you, hear you, and see your power."

"Oh God, I'm scared."

He gasped, opening his eyes. With his mouth still on her shoulder, he licked the bite, sealing it.

They were both silent, and then he gently pulled from her body and lay over her, his one thigh between her thighs. He reached up and caressed her hair from her cheek as he held her gaze. She looked shocked, and he wasn't certain if what he saw, felt, and experienced actually happened.

"Adrian?"

"Was it real?" he asked, and she nodded and then pulled her bottom lip between her teeth. "Holy shit, it was incredible, Salina. I felt all of you, your soul, your true self, and the power within you. The connection was so strong. I'm fucking shocked right now, lassie."

She chuckled. "You're shocked? I feel like I've entered the Twilight Zone. In a matter of days I've found out that wolves and wizards and even vampires exist, that I have some kind of power passed down by my parents who were some kind of wizards or Magi, and six Alpha males are biting me and marking me so we are bound for eternity."

"Wait, hold on a second. Your father was a wizard, and your mother what? You know about this power you have?" he asked.

She swallowed hard. "My father told me a few things. But I still don't know what power it is I have. It's strange, but every time one of you has bitten me, I feel like this shield or barrier inside is weakening and the power within me is growing stronger. I've never felt so much emotion in my life."

"I felt it, too. I could sense the shield, but then it weakened after I marked you. It must be some kind of protection. There are things going on that are concerning all of us. Until we know exactly what powers you possess, Salina, we need to protect you. That's why we're taking you with us to Ireland."

* * * *

"Ireland? Are you out of your mind? I can't go to Ireland. I have a life here, a job, open homicide cases to handle."

"Calm down. It will all be taken care of."

"By whom?"

"By people placed all over this area in different positions to do just this. Make you disappear without anyone taking notice. We have it all planned out."

"Get up. Let me up," she demanded, and he did. He stood up, looking confident and sexy in all his glorious assets and muscles as his cock tapped against his belly. He was huge, and hard again. How was that possible? She still couldn't get over how big her men were in all aspects of the word. Her belly quivered and a need, that itch of hunger, tingled deep in her core. She swallowed hard.

She was calling them her men. She submitted to them, to Adrian stating he was her Alpha. Saying, even thinking that word did something to her deep inside. But she was human as far as she knew. She didn't understand all this culture and ways of the wolf. Now they wanted to take her out of the country to their homeland?

"What are you thinking? Talk to me, lassie, and we'll work it out together. I can explain anything you need to know."

"I'm not leaving. Not now, and there isn't even a reason why I have to. I'm not in danger. No one has tried anything."

"Jeremiah? Do you recall the fucker's tongue down your throat and his hands on your ass, because I fucking do." He raised his voice, his fists by his side, his thick brogue more defined with anger. They all got that way when they were pissed. No person in their right mind would want to be on the receiving side of their anger.

"Adrian, that was intense, but he was just a pushy guy who thought he could take what he wanted."

"It was more than that," Brady stated firmly from the doorway. He walked in as she grabbed Adrian's shirt from the bed and pulled it on.

Adrian pulled on his kilt and she realized that he didn't in fact wear any underwear under it. Her cheeks warmed and her pussy leaked. *Get a grip, woman. These men want to control your life and take you out of the country. You need to slow them down.*

"Brady, please. I'm not in any danger. I have a professional life here. I can't just leave. Reggie and I have a case we're working on. In fact, I think it's time I head to my place for some clothes and to check messages. I don't even know where my cell phone is." She looked around the bedroom where she'd spent at least two days. She pushed her hair to one side as she looked around by the chair near the bed. She never even went to work. Reggie was going to tease her relentlessly.

She was lost in chaotic thoughts when Brady grabbed her hand and pulled her against his chest. One arm wrapped around her and he placed his hand on her ass under the shirt as he pressed her body against his. His thick, hard muscles pressed against her, making her feel feminine and sexy. The feel of his warm hand on her ass against her skin as he trailed a finger between the crack of her ass and his scent consumed her body. She practically moaned, and that hungry feeling throbbed within her. He looked down into her eyes as she held onto him.

"You are in danger. You don't understand because you don't know anything about these types of wolves and what they're capable of. There are things going on."

"What things?"

"We'll discuss it with you downstairs with the others. Our staff is cooking up lunch before we head to the airport." She pulled from Brady. He looked wild, his green eyes piercing as he stared at her, making her body hum with need. She had to stand her ground despite his intimidating demeanor.

"I'm not leaving the country. What about my father? He'll worry. I need to see him and ask him questions. I have a life here, damn it." She raised her voice and both men crossed their arms in front of their massive chests. She wasn't an idiot. She knew it wasn't smart to challenge these men who could shift to wolves and bite her. Hell, she saw Jeremiah's instant change from man to wolf. If Brady hadn't stepped in along with Adrian, then she would have been in a worse situation.

She turned around and walked toward the bed, crossing her arms and trying to think of a response to their demands. But that sensation brewed within her belly. That itch, that knowing voice that said she needed them and she should not fight their control. It was too fucking difficult for her to relinquish hold to men she really didn't know. Sure she had sex with them and it was amazing, but to give up her life, and just accept their orders and demands, was incomprehensible as far as she could understand.

She took a deep breath and then released it. Her mind fogged her negative thoughts, her fear of letting go of the control.

They were right. She didn't know anything about their kind or their capabilities. How would she learn? The hard way? She was caught between dealing with things on her own the way she was used to, and accepting the word of men who shifted into wolves on a snap of their emotions' or their minds' decision. She didn't even know how it worked. Did it hurt? Did they always appear back after shifting in full human form and naked?

The thought of their sexy, muscular bodies caused that itch-like feeling to tingle under her skin. When she felt the heavy, large hands wrap around her waist from behind, she gasped only for Brady to hold her tighter. He kissed along her neck.

"Relax," Brady said. "I can practically see the wheels turning in your head. You need to trust us. We made love to you, we are working on binding our souls. We are never going to abandon you, leave your side, or dismiss what is shared between us. I know it's all new but you must accept our command."

"We are your Alphas. We are in charge and people and wolves respect us. You will do the same," Quinn added, joining Adrian and Brady in the room with her.

She looked at him as he stepped in front of her. Here she was again, squeezed between two men she hardly knew but gave her body to fully.

"I'm sorry, but I'm not used to this. I've always had to prove my capabilities in life and in my profession. I don't appreciate being treated like some servant or unequal partner."

Quinn raised one eyebrow at her. She knew the servant comment was a bit harsh, but she was feeling on the defensive. This was natural and these men-wolves were damn intimidating.

Quinn placed his hand against her cheek.

"Servant? Never. An equal, of course, in love and companionship, bound for eternity. You are part of us as we are part of you. But we are Alphas, the most powerful, dominant of all wolves. You must accept our power and authority, our control, and respect it, or your life and our future could be in jeopardy."

She felt her gut clench and instincts kick in or something telling her that what they said was true. She may need to tone down her feminist attitude just slightly and show these men she cared for so deeply, maybe even felt love for already, that she indeed respected them and was working on trusting them and their judgment. But it wasn't easy. Inside she fought for the control she felt she always had. With these men, her mates supposedly for life, they were demanding that she relinquish that control over to them. She wasn't sure she could. It would be like giving up her identity and who she really was, or at least thought she was, until now. Why hadn't her father explained things sooner? What was with the shield, and how important were these powers she supposedly possessed? Her mind ranted and raved in questions as Quinn, Adrian, and Brady waited for a response from her. She took a deep breath, absorbed their good looks, their sincerity, and masculinity.

She took a deep breath and released it.

"I'm trying here. I want to trust you, but it's difficult for me because of the independence I've had for so long."

"We're not asking you to give that up, we're asking for you to trust us, and to accept our authority and care. Please, Salina, we can't lose you. Life would be over for all of us," Quinn said as Brady kissed her neck.

"I'll try, Quinn. I'll try."

Quinn caressed her cheek and gave her a quick kiss and then Brady turned her around in his arms and held her gaze firmly.

"Your Alpha is in need of a kiss from his woman."

He was trying to tease her and lighten the moment, but she knew Brady. He was tough, determined, and wild. Plus, he saved her from being hurt by Jeremiah.

She leaned up on her tiptoes, ran her hands through his hair, and gripped it best she could considering it was short, and she kissed him.

Chapter 12

Torque stood by the terrace looking out over the city. He couldn't believe it. Athlena had a child with that weak half-breed wizard Pierce. *How could I not know? How was that hidden so well from me? Salina is even more special then I sensed. There is magic guarding her, which could only mean she is definitely very valuable. I need to know what she is. She may be more valuable than I first thought. That means she is worth more, and Carbarone will pay a high price. She can also help to protect me from being captured.*

"Any news from your sources about Salina?" Carbarone asked as he joined him on the patio off the balcony.

"Actually, it seems your little prize is quite a bit more important than even I had thought."

"What do you mean?" Carbarone asked.

"There was some kind of magic blocking me from viewing her completely. Since leaving the party, and having the two days since it to think of her more, it hit me."

"Well, tell me. I need to know how much of an asset she will be to our pack. Jeremiah can't wait to have her."

"Her mother was a Magi. She had many abilities, but the strongest was her ability to read minds, and to see people for what they truly were."

"For real?"

Torque nodded.

"Why hadn't anyone snagged her mother up for themselves?"

"First, she fell in love with a half breed. Half wizard and half human. Very weak, but they were intended mates. She deserved much better than him. She was quite a beauty just as her daughter is."

"You sound like you were interested in her and knew her well."

"I did." Torque turned away from Carbarone and looked out toward the night sky.

"We would have been very powerful together. But she wouldn't join my efforts in overthrowing the Circle of Elders as well as the leader of the Magi. It would have brought us immense power. But no. Not Athlena. She wanted the simple life, she wanted to mate with that half breed, and she did. She disappeared until…"

"Until what?"

Torque turned to look at Carbarone. His heart raced with such anger and disgust. Torque could have gotten away with assisting the demon in trying to destroy the Goddesses of the Circle, but Athlena emerged among the fighters. She, along with other wizards and Fae, fought against the evil. It had come down to his life or hers. Torque had desired Athlena, perhaps even loved her, but she faced him in the battle and he won.

Torque looked at Carbarone. "No need for you to worry about it. Just know that she will be a great powerful asset to your pack and the fight against the Circle. She can assist you in taking over Skylar Pack. Her powers and abilities, especially if she is unaware of them, can be influenced and directed by you and me. You need to make a move, to do something that will get her to accept your nephews as her mates."

"Like what? What would you suggest?"

"A clear and firm threat."

"She has no family, but her partner, Reggie, could prove to be useful in this type of situation."

Torque shook his head. "I was thinking something that would really get Salina to submit to them. Like perhaps hurting her father."

Carbarone's eyes widened. "I like your way of thinking, Torque. I'll have my men take care of this, and be sure that Salina is notified. That should also pull her out of hiding."

"Indeed, and then your nephews can force the mating upon her and make her succumb to them. You'll take over Skylar Pack, and the Circle, the goddesses, and even Lord Crespin will take you more seriously than ever before."

"I like the sound of that. Let's do it now. The sooner I take over Skylar Pack, the stronger I will be, especially with you, Torque, a very powerful wizard, by my side."

"Of course. It's what we've planned all along, hasn't it been?"

Carbarone nodded his head and headed back inside.

Torque closed his eyes and thought of Athlena and then Salina.

"Perhaps the tables will turn, and just maybe I'll keep Salina all to myself."

* * * *

Delaney and Eagan both felt antsy. Especially now that they heard from Reggie and it seemed that Salina's lieutenant was working with Carbarone. Angus contacted Task Force Eight, the Lawkins Pack, and spoke directly to their Alpha, Blaise.

"They said they will place some watchers on them immediately. Hopefully that should provide a buffer in protecting Salina," Angus told them.

Delaney looked at Eagan then at Angus. "I don't like the fact that Jeremiah took an interest in her."

"None of us do," Quinn stated.

Angus's phone rang again. This time it was Vanderlan.

"Yes." Angus placed the phone on speaker just as Salina and the others entered the room. She was only wearing a shirt but was swimming in it.

Eagan pulled her into his arms and inhaled her scent. It calmed his wolf. Then Delaney brushed his thumb along her lower lip before giving her a small, quick kiss.

"It seems that the Carbarone pack are in fact interested in mating with your woman," Vanderlan said.

A series of "whats" went through the room.

Sal tried to step away from Eagan but he pulled her back against him. He kept his arm firm and snug against her waist and he softly whispered into her hair near her ear.

"Don't step away from me. I need you close."

He felt her ease back against him and then exhale. He glanced at Delaney, who winked but held a firm expression as Vanderlan explained his statement.

"Received the heads-up from Samantha that Jeremiah Carbarone is claiming you have stolen his intended mate. He said that he and his brothers saw Sal first, that Jeremiah kissed her, and she submitted to his advances and that Brady and Adrian threatened to kill him."

"What a load of bullshit. That fucking dipshit wouldn't know what to do if I had threatened him," Adrian responded.

"This is nonsense. Who cares what Jeremiah claims? It's obvious that Salina is our intended mate. You can't just go around claiming women as such," Brady said with his hands on his hips.

"Unfortunately for you guys, the elders, two in particular who claimed to take it seriously enough, have ordered your appearance before the board."

"Bull-fucking-shit!" Brady roared.

Eagan felt his temper rise, too.

"Calm down, Brady," Angus ordered.

"We are not leaving our mate to go to some stupid meeting to prove she is in fact ours," Delaney exclaimed.

"Listen, you should receive the call soon. They will tell you when and what time to be at the location they choose. The Circle of Elders will make a decision based on both sides. I'm certain when they hear the facts and also learn of your mating, the case will be dropped. You are moving forward in the mating process, are you not?" Vanderlan asked.

All eyes fell upon Salina and she straightened out her shoulders. Eagan chuckled as he smoothed his palm a little higher, just grazing the underside of her breast. It was torture trying to keep from bending her over the island and having his way with her. He and Delaney needed to mark her, too.

Salina covered his hand with hers and gently lowered it.

"We most definitely are," Delaney stated and winked at Salina.

"Then you need to go to the meeting. With your scents on her she should be okay staying here, along with some backup. Perhaps they will pick somewhere close by for the meeting?" Vanderlan told them.

"Do you think they would choose someplace far away from New York?" Angus asked.

"Ireland would be perfect," Brady said in a rough, angry voice with his arms crossed in front of his chest.

"It may take place outside of the city, and Salina will not be allowed to attend the meeting. She is considered unknown at this time, and since she is also considered human, the elders will not allow her anywhere near where they are."

"This is bullshit!" Eagan exclaimed, and Salina tightened up. He pulled her back against him and he kissed her neck. "Sorry, love, sometimes Were laws and rules can be a bit of a hassle."

"When we get the call and confirm a time and location, then we'll make plans to have security for Salina," Angus said and looked across the room at her. He gave her body the once-over. "We may need you, Vanderlan, and the rest of Task Force One to protect Salina."

"Of course. We can get to you within a few hours so just call us and we will head your way. I am certain that Dani would love to meet your mate sooner rather than later anyway. I'll be in touch. Good luck," Vanderlan said before he disconnected the call.

"Who is Dani?" Salina asked.

Eagan turned her around and caressed her cheek as he looked down into her eyes. Leaving her, even if only for a short period of time, would be difficult.

"We all feel the same way. But at least with our cousins protecting her we know that she will be in good hands," Angus stated through their mind link.

"Dani is mate to Vanderlan, who was just on the phone, and five Alpha wolves, Van, Miele, Randolph, Bently, and Baher," Eagan told her.

"Why is she so interested in meeting me?" Sal asked him.

Angus looked at his brothers and then back to Salina. "She was very good friends with our first mate, Margo."

Salina swallowed hard and he could see the concern and sadness in her eyes. She felt uncomfortable with that.

"Margo was a healer just as Dani is. It was Margo who protected Dani and helped to secure Dani's identity and block out any chance of her powers being detected," Delaney added.

"So Dani is a healer? Does it mean what I think it does?"

"Yes. She has the power to heal those who have been injured. She helped to heal her mates when they fought in a battle to protect her," Quinn stated.

Eagan pulled her closer and caressed his hand under her shirt and over her ass. He knew he exposed her rear to his brothers, but he was so in need of her, his wolf was becoming impatient. She reached back and tried to pull the shirt down.

"Eagan," she reprimanded, but he covered her mouth and kissed her. Soon her hands loosened and then she reached up and ran them through his hair.

He caressed her, causing her skin to be exposed. His brothers watched him intently.

"Your skin is so soft and silky. I love exploring you with my hands, but more so with my mouth." He lifted her up, she straddled his legs, and he carried her out of the room. Delaney was on his heels.

* * * *

Salina kissed Eagan as he carried her out of the kitchen. She knew the others watched and it turned her on, aroused her in a way she enjoyed feeling. Never in her life had she felt so sexy, so feminine and desired. When these men looked at her with hunger in their eyes, it fed an inner desire, as well as that burning need deep within her.

"You feel it, don't you, mate?" Delaney asked as she pulled her mouth from Eagan's and locked gazes with Delaney. Her breathing was rapid, and she felt an ache of need from what seemed to be every part of her body.

"Yes. It's crazy and I never felt anything like this before. Every time one of you are near I need so greatly it burns inside."

Eagan handed her to Delaney as Eagan pulled her shirt off of her.

She was naked in Delaney's arms. "You're so fucking beautiful, Sal, and we are going to ease that ache. We're going to mark you ours and seal our fate, our lives together. You got my dick so fucking hard." Delaney covered her mouth and kissed her deeply. She felt his emotions, and her mind raced for answers as it explored his mind.

She ran her fingers through his shoulder-length hair and gripped him tight. He had such a strong spirit. His desire for her, his attraction was so strong and so very real. He loved her breasts. He wanted to lick and nibble on her nipples. She felt her body release a small eruption. She pulled from his mouth.

"I need you. I want you. My breasts ache." She told him. His eyes widened and he hauled her up a little higher so he could feast on her breasts, a lick to the tip and then a small tug. She moaned out in pleasure.

"I'm ready," Eagan said, and then Delaney moved his mouth to her other breast, licked the nipple, and pulled it gently between his teeth as he flicked his tongue at the tip.

"Oh God, Delaney, that feels so good."

He released her breast and then nipped at her skin in a playful manner. "I fucking love your breasts, lassie. I could explore them for a while, but Eagan is in desperate need of a little pussy."

His words turned her on and she felt the gush of cream leak from her pussy. He licked her lip and then nibbled a hardened bud before he turned her around and placed her over a very naked and aroused Eagan. Delaney's words had her wet and ready for her lovers.

"Take me inside of you, Salina," Eagan told her. "Take of me whatever you want and need." He caressed his hand under her hair and cupped her head. She reached down and aligned his cock with her pussy. She stroked the thick, hard ridge of muscle, then cupped his scrotum.

"Oh damn, you little brat. Stop teasing me," he complained, and she smiled.

It felt so hard and thick. She sensed the anticipation, so she stroked his cock before teasing her pussy with the tip.

"You like that, baby? You like to tease your mate?"

She held his gaze. Eagan's blue eyes darkened as he gripped her hips and raised her slightly, indicating he'd had enough of her games.

"I like the way it feels, rubbing back and forth over my clit. Don't you?" She was feeling sexy and brazen. She was getting used to her lovers, and she prayed that they were truly bound together for life. She would never need or want for anything else or anyone else.

"I'll have to remember that. But right now, my cock is so fucking hard, baby, I need to be inside of you to ease this ache." She felt hands on her shoulders and then warm breath at the top of her head, just as Delaney pressed against her.

She gasped, feeling his thick, hard cock press to her puckered hole.

"I need you, too. I'm going to fuck this ass while Eagan fucks that sexy, wet pussy, love. We're going to make love to you together and fill you with Alpha cock."

"Yes, yes, do it. I need you both." She moaned and then lifted up and took Eagan inside of her. She lowered onto his shaft and tried to take him all in at once but she couldn't. Her desire, her hunger was great, but Eagan was thick and long. She had to ease him inside of her until finally their bodies collided.

Up and down she rode Eagan as he played with her breasts and pulled on her nipples. She closed her eyes and sensed his thoughts. She was getting better at doing this. It must be part of her powers.

She saw him in the heat of battle. A warrior just like his brothers, he fought for the good of wolves and of mankind. She sensed his strong love for her and it brought her such happiness she leaned down and kissed him.

"I adore you, Eagan. I feel it, too." She kissed him again. He squeezed her to him, and then she felt Delaney's tongue licking and arousing her anus. His hands spread her cheeks as he stroked his tongue and then pressed a digit into her ass.

"Oh God, Delaney!" she called out as she pulled her mouth from Eagan's.

Eagan held her tight. She couldn't move. "Nice and easy, mate. We're going to fill you up."

She felt Delaney pull fingers from her ass, and then she felt the tip of his cock at her back entrance.

Eagan lifted her hips and then pressed her back down as she thrust along with him. When she felt Delaney push through the tight rings, she remained still and relaxed her muscles, just thinking about the wonderful sensations she would feel once Delaney was seated fully inside of her.

Delaney worked his cock into her ass, and when she felt a plop sensation, she moaned along with Eagan and Delaney.

Smack.

She gasped.

"Fuck, I love this ass," Delaney said and then squeezed her ass cheeks, smacked the left cheek and then the right cheek before he thrust in and out of her anus.

She screamed her first release. "You're so wild," she told them.

"You make us wild. Fuck yeah," Delaney said then gripped her hips as he stroked his cock into her ass, and Eagan thrust up into her cunt.

"She is gorgeous. Too fucking beautiful to not fill up completely," Adrian said, joining them on the couch.

She felt her heart racing and her body was tight as a bow ready to break as Delaney and Eagan began to set a pace fucking her together. She heard Delaney's distorted voice.

"Look to the right, mate. Your Alpha needs that mouth of yours."

She turned to the right, moaning and grunting as Eagan and Delaney thrust into her together one after the next. "Oh." She moaned as she saw Adrian holding his thick hard cock with pre-cum on the tip. He held her gaze with molten fire in his eyes.

"I want to feel that sexy mouth."

He reached for her, taking a fistful of hair at the base of her head, and gently he guided her head toward his cock. She was aroused and hungry as she licked her lips and felt her nipples harden. Then she took a deep breath, tried to calm her excitement, and licked the tip.

Smack.

"Oh," she said as Adrian gently pressed his cock into her mouth.

She was shocked that Delaney had smacked her ass, and she was also turned on.

"No teasing. It will cost you. Remember that, mate. We're your fucking Alphas," Delaney said as he thrust into her harder, faster. She was sucking on Adrian and feeling full and so erotic she could sense her release coming hard.

She thrust her ass back against Delaney and it cost her a series of five smacks to her ass. "Fuck!" Eagan roared as he shot his seed up into her pussy and he held her tight. He leaned up and bit her shoulder, making her moan against Adrian's cock. She felt this burning sensation fill her body as if it traveled through her bloodstream. She sensed her body tingle, like something was happening inside of her.

"This fucking mouth. I love it. It's a damn weapon, lassie," Adrian said then ejaculated. She sucked and swallowed his cum and felt that tingling sensation increase. His scent, the taste of his essence caressed over her like a wave of power and protection. She was in awe of the sensations and connection.

He pulled from her mouth and fell backward on the couch with his arm over his eyes.

Delaney pumped faster. He gripped her around her midsection and moved so quickly she felt herself losing control. In her mind she saw all six of her men, standing beside her in wolf form.

"Come with me, mate. Come now, Salina!" Delaney ordered, and she exploded as he held himself within her and roared. When he bit into her shoulder, marking her, her head spun, her body convulsed, and she screamed out in ecstasy.

She fell forward, and darkness overtook her vision.

What happened? Why do I feel like this?

Can they hear me? Did I pass out?

She was filled with questions and then came the series of images in her head. Her powers were revealed. Her mother's bloodline, combined with the influence of her father's. She could read minds. She could decipher good and evil. She was a hunter of those whose souls were taken by a dark, evil force. Her mission was to bring killers to justice, to hunt down the monsters responsible for preying on the innocent and victimizing them. She was an angel on earth sent from the highest powers beyond the realms. Her destiny became clear.

I am an angel of earth and I seek justice for all those who were ripped of their lives and their innocence. My mates are my soldiers in arms, my protectors, and my enforcers. The gods and goddesses have spoken, and I am not the only angel of the gods.

* * * *

"Salina? Salina, are you okay?" Delaney asked as tried to wake her up.

She started to moan and he released a sigh of relief.

"Thank God she's okay. That was so weird. Her eyes rolled back in her head and then she jerked backward," Eagan added. He was caressing her hair from her face. Eagan had her cradled in his arms and now the others were there, too.

"What happened?" Brady asked, sounding angry.

"I don't know. It was so odd. I felt a force of some kind. Like some intense spark," Eagan told Brady.

"Yeah, I felt it, too. It didn't hurt but it was strong," Delaney said as Salina began to gain consciousness.

"She's human even if she does contain some Magi blood. She's still not an Alpha wolf. You need to be more careful with her," Angus roared from the doorway.

Delaney swallowed hard. He felt badly, but he would never harm Salina. Not ever. "I would never hurt her. None of us would. Something happened." He looked at her.

"Delaney?" she whispered, and he knelt down by the couch and took her hand into his own. Delaney brought it to his cheek and rubbed it against his skin.

"Yes, lassie. Are you okay?"

She smiled. "More than okay."

"Maybe she needs some rest. Carry her up to the bedroom to lie down," Angus ordered.

She looked at him as Eagan helped her to sit up. Delaney swallowed hard.

"I don't need a nap," she told them.

"I say otherwise. You passed out, doll. You need some rest, and no more pushing yourself. We give it a rest," Angus ordered.

"I said I'm fine. Won't you listen to what I have to say?" she asked, raising her voice.

"You will. You passed out, so that's telling me that your human body can't take the overload of wolves yet."

Delaney saw the argument coming, but then she shocked even him, never mind Angus. "No, Angus. You're wrong." She reached for the T-shirt. Delaney watched the material cover her sexy body. He couldn't help the feelings of disappointment he felt. He would love to have Salina walking around naked all day and ready for lovemaking. Then he felt tightness in his chest. Could he have really hurt her somehow?

"No, Delaney. You didn't hurt me. In fact, now that each of you have bitten me, marked me or whatever you like to call it, my identity and powers have been revealed."

"Wait, you heard my thoughts?" Delaney asked.

* * * *

Salina knew they would be shocked. Hell, so was she, but Angus was truly being combative and hard.

"You heard him?" Angus asked, stepping forward.

"You know what powers you have?" Brady asked.

She took a deep breath and released it. "I guess since my six mates have bitten and marked me, my powers have been revealed and I basically understand my role now. It's crazy, but it's kind of similar to my law enforcement profession."

"What are you talking about?" Quinn asked as he approached the couch. They were all surrounding her.

"You're part of it, too. Like my backup," she teased.

"Salina, explain," Angus ordered in that damn bossy tone of his.

She told them about her vision and about feeling the power of her abilities.

"So you can read minds?" Angus asked. She watched him, sensing that the ability definitely freaked him out. As she watched, she heard what he was thinking. He felt she was in danger. He felt he wasn't good enough for her and was unable to protect her. He felt that way because he believed that he failed Margo. She looked at the others. Their fears were similar in that they were worried about protecting her. They feared losing her and wanted to be protective.

"Listen, I understand that it has been difficult to lose your first mate. No insult intended, but I am not Margo. My role is clear now. I am an angel of the earth. I am here to stop evil from succeeding. I protect the innocent and bring justice to victim's families by finding their killers and locking them up or eliminating them. And guess what? You six are my trusty sidekicks."

They all just stared at her in shock.

"Okay, maybe trusty sidekicks wasn't the right way to describe your positions. I guess you're like my own personal protectors as I engage in these investigations into finding the bad guys and taking them down. It's so much like my real job, and it feels right."

"This is a lot to take in. Reading minds, risking your life as you hunt killers. Are you certain?" Brady asked.

She nodded her head.

"If I close my eyes, there's more information for me. I'm totally behind in my investigations, and get this, there are more like me. They, too, are hidden within this world and others."

"You mean realms?" Quinn asked.

"Whatever. It's important that you understand that this is my destiny. I'm not quitting my job. I am certainly not going to Ireland right now, and I am definitely bringing down the ones who killed Margo."

She stood up and Eagan let his hands slide down her thighs.

"So you have the ability to read minds, you're an angel on earth sent by the gods and goddesses to find killers, and we're your security?" Adrian asked, sounding totally annoyed.

"That about sums it up. There's so much to do. You know what, Angus, maybe I will lie down for a while. Perhaps as I sleep, more information will come to me." She smiled but the men still seemed perplexed.

"This is so great. It's a lot like my profession now. I can't wait to learn more."

* * * *

"Hold it right there. We need to talk about this, and figure things out. I, for one, haven't heard of such a thing existing. Now maybe it's only here in America, but since there are shithead criminals everywhere, it shouldn't matter where you are."

"I don't know, Angus. I guess that makes sense." Salina sat back down on the couch next to Eagan, who was now dressed in only his jeans. Delaney was pulling on his shirt.

"Why wouldn't we know it was our calling, too, then?" Brady asked her.

She took a deep breath and seemed to think about it a moment. "I don't know. I'm thinking that the stronger the bond builds between us, the more information I will get and the more I learn to understand my full purpose. However, I do get this feeling that I'm not fully empowered. It's like, I don't know, a sensation in my gut that seems to feel I'm not ready. Maybe even vulnerable? Does that make sense?"

"Sure it does. Considering that you can read people's minds, I'd say there would be lots of bad people who'd want to exploit your abilities, maybe even use you for evil," Brady said.

"That does make sense. You're probably in your most vulnerable state now as you're breaking down the shield placed on you to protect you," Quinn said.

"But no one but the six of you know what I am and what my powers are, so shouldn't I be safe?" she asked.

"No. You're not safe, in fact, you're in greater danger than I initially thought. Leaving for Ireland as soon as we can is our best choice. We can protect you there, on our homeland and amongst our packs."

"No. I'm not leaving here. Ireland is not where I'm supposed to be," Salina stated as she stood up and placed her hands on her hips.

"You will do what I say. You don't even know where you're supposed to be," Angus countered.

"Well, it's not as a prisoner in your home in Ireland. I belong on the streets doing my job. I need to see my father. I need to explain and then perhaps he'll have answers for me as well."

Before Angus could reply his cell phone rang. "It's Gideon." Angus answered the elder and they made arrangements to meet in two hours. He disconnected the call.

"We need to call Fagan Pack. Our session before the elders is in two hours. It's upstate, so we'll need to leave in fifteen minutes."

"All of us?" Brady asked.

"Yes. Get Reggie on the line. He'll need to stay here with Salina and guard her. We'll notify Fagan Pack, and they can make their way here," Angus ordered.

Quinn pulled Salina into his arms and hugged her.

"You listen to Reggie. You don't leave this house for any reason at all unless it's burning down."

"I understand. I'll wait for you," she said, and Quinn kissed her. Angus watched his brothers each give her a thorough kiss, and then he stared at her. She held his gaze. A new, stronger, more assertive woman stood before him. She was his equal. He understood that. She wasn't anything like Margo. But her importance to the Were world and to humans was revealed. She was destined for greatness.

Could he find it in himself to take the chance to love her and to get close to her and protect her as she would need? He prayed to the gods that he could. But first he needed to put those Carbarone assholes in their place.

"Come here," he told her. She took a deep breath and then walked closer. He gripped the T-shirt she wore, and his wolf grew hungry for her body that was naked underneath the flimsy cotton.

"You obey me. You remain here guarded and with Reggie. We will settle this situation with Carbarone and then work on the plan to head back to Ireland. You are the mate to six exceptional Alphas who have a job to do. If what you say is true and we are in fact destined to be your guards, then let's resolve this current issue so we can work on our mating, and our future."

"I understand."

He held her gaze and pulled her closer before kissing her deeply.

When their lips touched, he felt her love for him, and it left him in awe of her power. Somehow he saw what she was thinking and knew that she felt good, proud of her power and her ability to help victims' families and bring justice to them all. He didn't mind one bit hunting evildoers. So maybe the gods got it right this time, and perhaps he could in fact protect his mate unlike the last time.

He released her lips and she held his gaze.

"Behave, or else."

She nodded, and he exited the room to prepare to leave.

Chapter 13

"Are you sure that this is going to work?" Jaydin asked Torque as they gathered around the meeting room.

"I am certain. Gideon is a moron. He fell for everything your uncle told him about Salina being your mate and not Fennigan Pack's," Torque said.

"Okay, here's the location of the house. The plan will set in motion as soon as Fennigan Pack arrives at the meeting place."

"And the guards assigned to watch Salina?" Jeremiah asked.

"She will be so worried about her father's safety none of them will matter. In fact, she more than likely will sneak out to get to her father so none of the security will matter. If Reggie goes with her, then we take him out, too. Our team of warriors will simultaneously invade the Skylar Packs both here and in Ireland. If they fight for the rights to it, then, Jaydin, you challenge him before the Circle of Elders," Torque told him.

"But what about the fact that we called this meeting and demanded justice be served and then we don't even show up?" Jeremiah asked.

"It's minimal nonsense. You can say that the takeover took precedence over confirming Salina as your mate. That you were ensuring her place beside you as you expanded your territory and challenged McCarthy Skylar for all his land in the US and Ireland."

"And what about Salina's father?" Jett asked.

"I'll handle him. It will be my pleasure," Torque said.

"And Salina will fight us as well," Jett stated.

"You inject her with this," Torque said. "The second you have the opportunity, you do it and you bring her to Ireland where the largest Skylar Pack land is. One of you mark her to wipe the scent of Fennigan Pack from her body. If they dare follow and challenge, then you three get your wish and you fight Fennigan Pack Alpha Angus to the death."

Jeremiah smiled. "I call marking her." He licked his lips and rubbed his hands together.

"I call killing Angus," Jaydin chimed in.

"Then I get to kill Reggie," Jett said, and they all smiled.

"Call the packs, get them in place. Our strike occurs in thirty minutes. Have your father prepare the jet. Oh, and have a backup plan in case we need to move quickly. I have the feeling that Fennigan Pack won't want to leave their woman's side for long. You may need to adjust the plan of attack at their home instead of at Salina's father's," Torque said.

"I've got it covered. We'll keep a team surrounding that house and ready to invade," Jaydin informed them.

"Everything is in place. Now we sit and watch them fall into the traps. I can't wait to get my prize, sweet Salina," Jeremiah said.

Torque smiled to himself. Things had a way of working themselves out. Having a woman like Salina with all her powers could indeed give Torque back the freedom that had been taken away from him.

* * * *

"Salina, you can't call your father and have this conversation over the phone. Are you crazy? Think about it, will you?" Reggie reprimanded Salina as she started punching in her father's phone number.

She stopped and looked at him. "I need to talk with him. He has to know what my powers are and he probably has some insight into them, too."

"Well, then let's send someone for him. That would make more sense."

"Well, what are you waiting for?" she asked.

A half hour later Salina was pacing the living room. "He should have been here by now. Did you call the men you sent?"

"Yes, and I didn't get an answer. Fagan Pack should be here soon."

"What can they do?"

Reggie thought about that a moment. "They can stop there and check things out to make sure that your father is safe. Perhaps the guards saw something they didn't like and needed to intervene." Reggie pulled out his cell and spoke with one of the men named Van. "Okay, they are going there first."

"Good."

They both looked up toward the ceiling at the loud noise that nearly rocked the house.

Reggie pulled out his gun and Salina reached for hers and then cursed as she realized her men had yet to return her weapons after they first arrived here.

"Just stay here."

"Fuck that. Let's go see what that noise was."

The alarms sounded a moment later as both Reggie and Salina began to climb the stairs.

The windows shattered, the room filled with smoke and then there was gunfire. "We're under attack!" Reggie exclaimed.

"You think? Hand me something. I don't even have a weapon."

"Run, Sal. Run to the master bedroom." He fired his gun at the wolves. Sal ran as fast as she could. She got to the top of the stairs and ran down the hallway. She thought she heard glass breaking, but just kept running until she got to the room. A quick glance over her shoulder and there was Reggie, eyes glowing, his teeth looking sharp and ready to tear someone apart. For a moment she wondered if he was coming for her, and then she read his thoughts.

"The closet. Get in to the closet, behind the case of ties is a secret compartment. There's an elevator that leads down to an exit through the gardens. Head that way and then take the first path to the right. Follow it for two miles until you reach a development."

On his last words she saw the men approach the top of the stairs. Sal ran into the room, went to the closet, and closed the door. She looked at the tie rack, pulled on it, but it wouldn't budge. She was frustrated and in a total panic when she started looking around it. She spotted a shotgun. She pulled it out, checked for ammo, and saw it was loaded. She reached around the rack again and the door opened. With the shotgun in hand and two shells inside, she headed into the small dark space. Sure enough, there was some kind of box thing with a down button. She got inside, sat legs crossed, and held the shotgun over her lap. Reaching out, she pressed the button as growls and howls filled the air.

The elevator went down and she prayed that Reggie was right. As it stopped in a pitch-black area, the doors opened and she could see another small tunnel with light at the end. She made her way out, heart pounding as she thought of her mates, but felt a stinging sensation instead. Her eyes felt different. She could see so clearly it was amazing.

She pushed the small door open and she was way in the back of the house in the center of the gardens. She climbed out and looked around with eyes so sharp and focused she was a bit scared. She could hear the wolves, the alarms wailing as if they were right nearby yet everything was black.

It was crazy but she could hear so clearly, too. Her body felt different.

She hurried out of the gardens and ran as fast as she could across the way until she reached the area where the developments were. Just as she decided which way to run, she heard a growl and cried out as a wolf tackled her to the ground. The gun fell to the grass and she screamed and then tried to reach for it.

"Don't hurt her." She heard a deep voice from a distance. Sal grabbed for the gun as two wolves growled near her. She pointed the gun and shot one wolf. He howled and then there were others. She only had one shot left. She got up to her feet and pointed around her. One more she could kill until the others got to her.

"Don't do it. It's over. You belong with us," one of them said as another jumped toward her as if it were going for the gun. Sal shot and the wolf went down.

Salina ran and in her mind she reached out to Reggie, to her mates, and felt nothing.

She screamed and then turned around only to see three other wolves standing in her way. They were growling low and she slowly started backing up. Her heart pounded inside of her chest and her breath caught in her throat. Strong arms wrapped around her waist and something pinched her neck.

"You're all mine now, Salina." She turned to see Jeremiah standing there holding a needle. Her vision blurred and her body went weak. She could hear Reggie yelling "no," but then Jeremiah was carrying her away and out of the house. She couldn't move a muscle and the last thing she thought about were Angus's words and her six Alpha mates.

"I need you. They're taking me away. Jeremiah stuck me with a needle. Help me please."

* * * *

"They're still not here. Isn't it obvious that they lied about Salina being their mate? She is ours, and we need to get back to her." Brady raged at the four members of the Circle standing there waiting on Carbarone.

Angus grabbed his head, his brothers closed their eyes, and everyone around them asked what was wrong.

"It's a trap. Salina has been abducted by Jeremiah Carbarone. They invaded our home," Angus said.

"Gideon, we just got a call from Ireland. Skylar Pack territory has been taken over by Carbarone. They are calling for a challenge to the Alpha McCarthy," one of the Beta guards informed them.

Angus roared and slammed his hand down on the table. "It's a damn trap and now our mate is in danger because of you."

* * * *

Brady and the others followed Angus out of the room.

"Holy shit, I heard her. She called to us for help," Eagan said, sounding shocked.

"We all heard her. We need to get to Salina," Delaney said. They ran from the building and headed toward the SUV.

"Get on the phone with Fagan Pack. Reggie isn't answering right now," Adrian said.

"We have to get to her, Angus. She needs us. There's no telling what Carbarone will do to her," Brady said, and Angus stepped on the gas and headed back to the estate.

By the time they reached the house, all hell had broken loose.

Vanderlan and Randolph were there to meet them as were firefighters and special cleanup crews, who began to secure the estate.

"What the fuck happened?" Angus roared.

"They took Salina," Vanderlan told them.

"We know. She somehow spoke to us, informed us that she was in trouble, and asked for help." Angus thought about that a moment. He didn't feel very good right now. In fact he was thinking that Salina might end up like Margo. Dead. He'd failed Salina already by leaving her side and making her vulnerable to an attack.

"Reggie is injured. Dani is with him now," Randolph informed them.

"Let's go see him, then figure out where they took Salina," Delaney said.

"We've got people working on that now, including Declan Pack. Ava ordered troops to go in and assist Skylar Pack. The word is that McCarthy has been injured," Randolph told them as they headed through the house.

Angus couldn't believe the mess. Windows were shattered, a dense fog of smoke filled the air, making it difficult to see, and there were bodies, men who had been on guard as protectors to Salina who gave their life trying to keep her safe. His gut clenched.

As they approached the upper floors, Angus spotted Miele, Van, Baher, and Bently. They all shook hands and then Bently informed Angus and his brothers about Reggie.

"We were on our way here when Reggie called and asked to check on Salina's father. We got to the house and saw that it was ransacked. Her dad was taken, too. We tried calling here, got no answer, so we headed this way but were too late. Dani said that Reggie might not make it. She got to him in time. They left him for dead, but there is some kind of spell over him. Dani doesn't trust it at all."

"Son of a bitch. I can't wait to get my hands on them. The Carbarone family is going down," Delaney said.

"We're with you on that," Miele said. "They basically bypassed Were authority and that of the Circle, lied to them to set up that fake meeting, and then abducted your mate and her father, then left Reggie for dead. Then of course there are the dozen or so guards they took out, too."

"Your team took out two dozen or more of Carbarone's men, so know they did put up a good fight to keep your mate secure," Bently told Angus.

"It has to end. We can't lose Salina like we lost Margo. We need to find out where they took Salina and her father," Angus told them.

"Reggie is awake but not for long. Dani gave him something to calm him," Van said as he stood by the doorway.

Brady, Angus, Delaney, Eagan, Adrian, and Quinn entered the room.

"Holy shit, he looks like hell," Adrian said as he approached first. He gave Dani a kiss on the cheek and she smiled.

"It was a close call. Thank goodness you all asked us to come and help," Dani said.

The others greeted her but Angus stood back.

Dani approached him and caressed his arm. "This isn't your fault. Just like Margo's death wasn't."

"I don't want to hear it, Dani. I failed Salina, too."

"No, you didn't. You marked her, mated her, and began the binding. She needs you more than ever right now," Dani told him.

"Angus, we just got word from Sean Declan. Jeremiah Carbarone boarded a private jet with Salina and her father. They're headed to Ireland," Vanderlan told them.

"That piece of shit. He wants to fight on our land, then so be it. Let's get the jet fueled and ready," Angus said.

"Already done, Angus. Go get your mate and bring justice to Margo's death once and for all," Van told him.

Angus smiled. "You bet your ass we will. Let's go, brothers, our woman needs her security team in place before we take out the bad guys once and for all."

Chapter 14

"You should have killed Pierce. You have the woman. We won't need him around to get her to do what we want," Jeremiah said as he looked at Pierce, comatose on the couch in the living room.

Torque glared at the man. He would like nothing more than to see the half-breed wizard dead, and maybe Jeremiah was right and keeping Pierce alive for a bit longer would cause a problem. Torque wasn't certain, but he did know that Salina would do just about anything for her father, her only blood relative.

"Make sure you keep him sedated. I'm not certain how strong his powers are and we don't need any surprises," Torque told Jeremiah. Jeremiah moved Salina's hair from her cheek.

"When can I have her? I want to mark her so when those fucking losers come they see she is mine and not theirs anymore. How long do I have to wait until I can play with her?" Jeremiah asked.

"Soon. When she awakens I need to test her powers. In the interim, check on Jaydin and Jett. See if they have control over Skylar Pack yet."

Jeremiah took out his phone.

"It was a great idea to load the weapons with silver bullets. McCarthy is injured and there's no way he can challenge my brother now."

"Yes, everything is coming together nicely."

* * * *

Salina listened to what they were saying. So this was some kind of planned attack on the Skylar Pack. They set her men up and prepared to kill them. She worried about Reggie and hoped that he was okay. She must have been unconscious a while to have made it to Ireland. How the hell did these men get away with it?

Her mind felt fuzzy, but then there was this sensation inside. Flashes of images scattered through her mind. Torque was a wizard, a man of powerful abilities. But he was also evil. His intentions were to destroy the power of the Circle. To manipulate the weak and think nothing of mass murdering innocents was despicable. For some odd reason she thought about her mother, and her untimely death. Why was she feeling like Torque had a hand in it, too?

"Playing possum will cost you, Salina," Torque said. He caressed her cheek and then sat next to her on the couch.

"She's awake?" Jeremiah asked.

She blinked her eyes open. She held their gazes. "What am I doing here? What have you done?"

"No questions. You're right where you belong." Torque placed his hands on her cheeks and closed his eyes. She felt the evilness collide against her body. A shield of some sort blocked him out and she didn't know where it came from but was grateful.

"Ahhh, very powerful indeed," he whispered, and she wondered how he could tell. Was he trying to place a spell on her? Did these wizards have the power of mind manipulation?

"You will succumb to the destiny I choose for you, Salina. You will mate with Carbarone and be theirs for eternity."

"No, I won't. I have mates."

"They will be dead soon enough, and even if they make it here, they will need to fight Carbarone for Skylar territory."

"They'll do it and then I'll kill you."

He chuckled. *"You have a strong spirit, Salina, but I am more powerful than you know. Plus, if you don't succumb to Jeremiah and his brothers, then your father will die, right here in front of you."*

He released her and looked toward her dad lying on the couch. She was amazed that Torque could speak to her in her mind, but she also had a feeling that she allowed it.

She looked at her father lying helpless and sleeping on the couch. His face was battered and bruised. Blood stained his ripped shirt. He was injured and seemed to have given the Carbarone men a fight before being captured. Something deep within her reacted to that.

She sat up, straightened out her blouse, and adjusted her pants. She stared at Torque and saw his plan, but then he shot her a look.

"A warrior angel. How intriguing," he whispered, looking her over.

"A warrior angel? What is that?" Jeremiah asked, moving closer.

Torque never took his eyes off Salina.

"She is an angel on earth, one sent to find and sentence those who have committed crimes like murder. She can read minds, as she just attempted to read mine," Torque told Jeremiah.

"That's pretty ironic, considering that she is a detective," Jeremiah said as he reached for her hair and caressed it. She pulled away and stared at Torque. "I didn't try to read your mind, I succeeded. Perhaps Mr. Carbarone, their uncle, would like to hear of your true plans?"

"Can I have her now?" Jeremiah asked as he walked closer. He was staring at her and she knew that look. An expression of hunger filled his eyes. He allowed her to see his wolf, and her body tensed, instantly on guard.

"First, what is the update on your brother and overtaking the territory?"

"He is in control. The only thing that could possibly stand in the way now would be for someone else to challenge him to Skylar Pack territory."

Jeremiah reached for her chin and she turned from his grasp. "I see you still need to learn about respecting your Alpha," Jeremiah told her.

"You're not my Alpha," she said slowly, feeling her hatred for this man intensify.

"There are no others. You belong to Carbarone Pack now, and you'll live here in Ireland on our newest claimed land."

She shook her head. "I don't belong to you."

"You don't know the rules and the laws of wolves. You belong to Carbarone Pack. Those weak Fennigan wolves gave you up. They left you and a wolf never leaves his mate. You will be ours shortly." Jeremiah pulled her up by her blouse, ripping the material. She lashed out at him and struck him across the face.

He shoved her down and climbed on top of her. He pressed his thigh between her legs and held her arms at her sides. She was no match for his wolf strength as she growled in anger from being so vulnerable and weak.

He smirked, letting his long, sharp teeth show.

"Don't fight it. It's no use," Jett said, approaching from behind the couch. He placed his hands over her shoulders, under her blouse, and cupped her breasts. Salina shook her head side to side.

"No! Get off of me. I don't want this."

"Allow me to assist," Torque stated and then moved closer.

"Of course you want to assist. You don't want them to know your plans. He is going to take over everything. He will control your minds and your uncle's, ultimately becoming pack leader," she said.

"She lies. Hold her still," Torque replied. She struggled to get free but it was no use. These men were megastrong. Jeremiah was breathing heavy. He looked like some caged animal and Jett's hands cupped Salina's breasts and squeezed them hard.

She wiggled and thrust upward, trying anything she could to get free.

"Hold her still," Torque said and then slapped his palm against her forehead, sending her head back against the couch.

She felt the sensation slam against her body. Something dark, hard, and mystical cascaded over her flesh.

"Accept them, Salina. Accept the Carbarone as your Alphas, and your father's life will be spared."

"No. You can't make me do this. You can't."

Salina heard her father's cry of pain and she screamed at Torque.

"Release him. Release him."

"Succumb to your fate. Allow Carbarone to bond with you, and your father shall live."

She cried as her father's torturous moans filled the room. She screamed out as tears rolled from her eyes.

"No. This isn't the way it's supposed to be."

Jeremiah licked her neck and then nipped at her skin. She shook and tried to fight him off.

"Fight him, Salina." She heard her father's voice. *"You are stronger than all of them. Believe in the gods and goddesses. Believe in your powers."*

Then Torque yelled out, forced his hands from Salina, and kept his palms forward toward her father.

Her father yelled out in pain and fell to the rug.

"Bite her now," Torque ordered.

"No!" she screamed as Jeremiah bit into her skin.

The pain was so terrible she screamed out in agony, and in her mind her men roared in anger.

"You belong to Carbarone now. Submit to him and his brothers or your father and your mates die," Torque threatened.

Her father moaned. In her mind she felt the defeat, she heard her mates roar in pain, and she feared for their lives, for her father's life.

Pain radiated in her shoulder. The blood oozed from her skin and Jeremiah licked it as he pressed his body against hers. She felt the tingling, burning sensation move through her blood. Jeremiah was of wolf and vampire. He was a killer, an evil criminal who took what he wanted. He, his brothers, and their father took females from their mates and tried to force the bond upon them just as he was doing to her now.

She saw the women who were taken, including two that belonged to the men who were murdered, the ones from her investigation.

"No!" She roared out as his blood seeped within her skin and she knew the combination weakened her. Were blood, vampire blood, wizard, angel, it was all boiling inside of her.

She felt Jeremiah's hands everywhere on her, against her breasts as he squeezed her and licked and suckled her skin.

She sobbed and felt her mates less and less as Torque chanted something. He was using some kind of spell or something and she was becoming weaker. She called out to her mates and then felt as if they had given up right before they left her mind. Suddenly she was empty.

"No," she sobbed.

"Yes. It worked. They are gone, dead to you now. Take your place where you belong." Torque ran his hands over her body and she felt a numbing sensation right before she closed her eyes and passed out.

Chapter 15

"Did you feel that?" Quinn asked as the pain struck his chest and he nearly faltered as he walked from the plane.

"All of it. I felt and heard all of it," Delaney replied.

"He fucking bit her. Jeremiah bit our mate," Brady said and then growled.

"We must get to her. Something blocked us from telling her we were on our way. It has to be Torque," Angus said.

"That fucker dies. I call fucking dibs on him," Adrian said.

"Only if I don't get my hands on him first, brother," Eagan added.

"We need to handle this accordingly. I don't trust Torque. His powers are strong and I think some extra backup might be in order," Angus said.

"I'm on it now," Brady replied and then pulled out his cell phone.

* * * *

"Ava, what exactly do you suggest we do?" Mick asked his mate as his brothers gathered around them. They were in the castle and word spread about the attack on Skylar Pack.

"I suggest you gather our troops and take it back," Ava replied.

"That's not exactly how it works," Sean added.

Ava looked at Sean and his piercing blue eyes. "Well, considering that the Carbarones haven't exactly been playing by the rules, I say go for it."

"Wait, Ava. I just got off the phone with Brady," Kyle told her. "Carbarone Pack has their mate. They took Salina. Now Jeremiah, with the help of Torque the wizard, is trying to break her binding. Jeremiah bit her."

Ava gasped and her men mumbled curses under their breath. She stared at them. "What does that mean exactly?"

"It depends on what Salina is, on any powers she may have. If they believe her to be a Magi and she couldn't resist and fight off Jeremiah, then they could be bound to her as well. There's no telling really," Sean stated.

"This is terrible. We need some more help. I'll call Kamea, and see who she can send immediately."

* * * *

"By the gods, please protect my daughter. Please help me to get her back. She'll die." Pierce felt his soul leaving his body. As he rose above it and stared down, he saw all the bruises and the blood and he wept. All his life he did what was asked of him. He served the gods and goddesses and avoided evil. He met and fell in love with his mate, Athlena, and accepted her abilities and vowed justice for her murder. He kept their daughter safe, and when her mates showed up, he accepted them and her fate as well. For they had suffered a similar loss that he had. They lost their first mate, a healer, and they knew how important it was to protect Salina.

This cannot end here like this. There must be more.

He tried his hardest to use the last bit of his strength. He called upon anyone in this realm or beyond who could assist.

"Please come help an angel of earth, a warrior sent here to protect the innocent and bring justice to victims, a woman so strong and powerful that she can hunt, locate, and destroy the evil that walks this earth. I need your help. Her mates need her and she needs them."

He stared at his body. Feelings of disappointment, failure, and emptiness filled his heart and soul.

"Fear not, my old friend. Your pleas have been heard by the goddesses. An army is forming, and you and your powers are greatly needed."

Pierce felt himself slowly ease back into his body. Somehow he didn't die, and his spirit didn't leave this earth. He felt the pain of his injuries again, and the heaviness in his heart. He looked up as the deep voice filled the air and a hand squeezed his shoulder making him gasp and remind him that he was still alive.

Tears filled his eyes and his heart leaped with joy.

"Feldman Sabonne, you crazy Fae Knight. Is it really you?" he asked. Feldman smiled. "I am as real as you are alive my friend. Let's go get your daughter, her mates have a hell of a fight ahead of them, and the others are gathering on the borders."

Feldman assisted Pierce with standing. "Others? Who else is coming to help?" Pierce asked as he looked around the room. He saw multiple guards lying on the floor unconscious or dead. He knew the Fae Knight had the ability to travel from realm to realm and go anywhere in a blink of an eye. This meant that the others knew what was happening. Help was on the way, and the fight wasn't over.

Feldman smiled. "Your daughter is the first Earth Angel to appear in this realm. It means the great battle against evil is present despite the changes in the Circle. Task forces are forming and your daughter will lead the way if we can get to her in time."

"Torque has cast a spell of some sort over her. She couldn't communicate with her mates because Jeremiah bit her, forcing a bond."

Feldman squeezed Pierce's shoulder. "The gods and goddesses have a plan, and we must allow Salina's destiny to play out. Let's move. We shouldn't keep Charity and her men waiting."

Charity?

Chapter 16

Salina stared at herself in the full-length mirror as three young women dressed her and applied makeup and body jewelry to her. She felt so out of body that she couldn't even speak and thinking, processing thoughts of where she was and why she was allowing this, brought pain to her forehead.

She was a modest person. She also was critical of her body, yet here she was fully exposed as women adorned her belly button with jewelry that attached to thin, gold-link chains around her neck and over her breasts. She looked like some exotic belly dancer, and then came the shear material. They placed her arms through the sleeves, soft, sheer, a cream color that was see-through. Even her arms felt weightless.

The material barely covered her breasts, which were abundant and felt full and aroused. The bottom of the dress gathered in the middle between her thighs, barely covering her pussy yet exposing her lengthy, tan, muscular legs.

One of the women nodded for her to step into the high heels. That was when she noticed the pedicure, fresh cream-colored nail polish and more thin, gold chains around her ankles.

She forced herself to think, to try and decipher what was real, and to feel, actually feel, her own body.

She reached out, nearly missing the young woman's arm. The young girl gasped and stared up into Salina's eyes.

"Where am I?" she asked.

In her mind she felt some sort of force field, some block or darkness that tried to manipulate her mind. She clenched her eyes tight and ground her teeth. Her grip tightened on the young woman. "Where am I?" she demanded.

The woman tried pulling away and Salina held on to her shoulder, and when her palm touched the woman's skin, Salina was struck with a vision.

In an instant she felt the young woman's emotions and heard her own story of survival. She was a slave, a servant to Carbarone. She had been taken from her mates in Skylar Pack and was going to be forced to mate with Vargon, but then Salina had arrived.

"Where is Carbarone now?" she asked.

"They wait for the ceremony. You're to be wed, mated to Jaydin, Jett, and Jeremiah Carbarone."

Salina felt a tingling on her shoulders. Flashes of her mates' bites, their marking, penetrated the wall around her body and soul. Salina shook her head.

"I am already mated."

The young woman shook her head. *"It doesn't matter. Torque the wizard forced a spell upon you. Jeremiah bit you and shortly they will force themselves upon your body and bind the spell."*

Salina shook her head as the sounds of howls filled the night outside the windows of the room.

The women cried and ushered her toward the door.

"They summon you now," another woman said.

"Who?" Salina asked as she yanked her arm from the woman's grasp.

"Your mates. They want you there to witness their takeover of Skylar Pack."

"What do you mean?" Salina asked, grabbing onto the woman's upper arm. She tried to pull away but Salina wouldn't release her hold. It was crazy, but she felt so powerful and strong. The dizziness, the feeling of being separate from her body, was lessening. "Explain it to me now."

Then she saw the woman's thoughts. She was informing Torque that Salina was no longer compliant to his spell. She saw the battlefield, the fighting that was taking place right outside this dwelling. Then she saw the men, the ones with silver bullets guarding Carbarone. They were cheating. They were using silver to kill the wolves, the innocent men, women, and children trying to protect their land.

She released her hold and felt intense pain hit her forehead. She knew it was Torque trying to challenge her resolve, and then behind the woman she saw the loveliest woman she had ever seen. Her image was pure goodness and she smiled.

"So it is true that an angel walks this earth. How wonderful."

"Who are you?" she asked in her mind even though there seemed to be a battle going on between Torque's power and her own.

"There isn't time to explain it all, but I am here to help you as much as I can. You have a very strong spirit. By Jeremiah forcing his bite, a binding, on you, you have received not only the blood of Were and vampire, but also wizard from Torque. You must believe that you are more powerful than any of them. For no one, angel, Were, vampire, or wizard alone could sustain what you have."

"I feel it. Yet, he is holding it back, controlling me. I don't feel whole," she whispered, the sensation of defeat giving Torque an added notch of control.

"You are stronger than him, than so many. I am friends with your true mates. They need you. They are battling now for control of the Skylar Pack territory after Torque and Carbarone defeated the Alphas with their use of silver."

"How can I help? He seems to have control over me."

"He has only the control you allow. You must believe in your abilities. You must understand that the title bestowed upon you is great, and that your abilities, your powers are needed to wean this world of evil killers. It is your destiny."

Salina cried out as a forceful pain shocked her system. She looked up as she screamed out loud and the woman was no longer there. The other women stared at her and then bowed their heads.

"You saw her, too?" she asked, cringing, feeling her body shake as she tried to resist Torque's hold.

One of the women nodded. "You can save us all. The Carbarones are coming now. They are going to bring you to the forefront of the battle and kill your mates before you. Then they will force the binding upon you and take you as their mate. Your powers will filter through them and they will then destroy the good, and other packs around Ireland and in the United States."

Anger and disgust filled her soul. She promised Torque that she would kill him. That was exactly what she was going to do.

She touched the woman's cheek and told her not to worry.

In her mind she pulled up a wall of power, something she suddenly realized she had the ability to do. It made Torque think that he had complete control over her mind and body, but beyond that wall information flowed from the gods and goddesses. Her blood tingled. Her heart pounded faster at the realizations filling her mind. She was indeed more powerful than many. When Jeremiah bit into her and took from her flesh, she gained the abilities of Were and vampire. When others would have died from the bite of a wolf not intended as a mate, she instead was able to pull from his powers, and combined with her own of Magi, wizard, and angel, she became even stronger, wiser, and more capable of her position. She was enforcer of the gods and goddesses. The challenges bestowed upon her were a test to her purity of heart and soul.

"I am here to stop the killings, to help all those who are weak and become victim to violence and evildoers. Carbarone Pack and Torque must be punished for their crimes, and if they resist, then they must die and leave this earth for eternity."

Chapter 17

"My brothers and I are humbled by your presence and support. Task Force Three, Task Force One, the Venificus brothers, all of your troops, and of course Princess Charity, we are humbled that you stand by our side," Angus stated to the crowd before him. Declan and Fagan Alphas stood in the front of the lines of soldiers. They were warriors ready to battle Carbarone and his men, as well as their weapons of silver.

"Skylar Pack has officially been overtaken by Carbarone Pack. Jaydin, Jett, and Jeremiah, along with their cousins and uncle, have gone to great measures to cause this destruction. They have lied, they have killed, and they have taken men's mates right from their grasps and done the unthinkable. Our own mate, Salina, is under the mind control of Torque the wizard. We are ready to take her back, and to overthrow these beasts and return to what is rightfully Skylar Pack territory."

The crowd roared with excitement. Angus raised his hand up. He glanced at Charity and the Knight Feldman.

"What Carbarone doesn't know is that we have the guidance and the support of the Princess of Malan, the Chosen one, and a great and powerful knight. The others, McCarthy included, went into battle head-on and realized too late that the enemy were fighting with silver."

Roars and grunted curses went through the crowd.

"I must warn you that this is their weapon of choice. They have no respect for the laws and regulations set forth by the Goddess of the Circle, the Ring, or the Circle of Elders. We officially received word moments ago, thanks to Ava, that the Circle of Elders, the Goddesses, and all royalty have agreed and asked that Carbarone and the wizard Torque, plus all associated with them, be placed under arrest and be prosecuted to the fullest extent of Were laws. My brothers Quinn and Delaney, who have composed a plan of attack, will now explain what each of you must do. Be brave, my friends, and remember our purpose. Salina represents an angel on earth, a keeper of the laws, and enforcer of them as well. If she dies, if we fail, then others will come and try to defeat the laws we all so strongly have fought to uphold." Angus motioned with his hand to Quinn and Delaney.

As Angus walked to the side, Charity and Feldman were there to greet him.

"You must stay focused and positive, Angus. Your mate's destiny depends upon it," Feldman told him.

"I failed her once. I don't expect to fail her again."

"You did not fail her," Charity said to him and then touched his arm.

He felt the vibration, like an electric current run under his skin along his arm, through his entire body.

"The gods and goddesses work in mysterious ways, Angus. Your mate, your angel on earth, needs you."

"It's important that you know these wolves will use anything to trick you. McCarthy is barely alive. Dani isn't sure she can save him. You need to believe that you and your brothers are meant to be with Salina and that together you will enforce the laws," Feldman said.

"We're all in this together. If Carbarone and Torque succeed, and Salina becomes their mate, then my brothers and I will leave. We'll give up our positions and eventually die. Without our mate, without Salina, we will not be able to go on in life, or in our positions as servants to the laws, to the Circle and the Brotherhood," Angus told them very seriously.

"You cannot give up. No matter how hard this fight is," Feldman said.

Angus looked toward his brothers as the crowds of people, friends, and fellow pack members gathered around prepared to do battle.

"Fennigan Pack fight until the death. This all ends here tonight."

* * * *

"I think we should start the mating right away," Jeremiah said and sniffed Salina's neck. He walked so closely behind her his body brushed against hers.

"She is definitely a valuable prize. By the gods, she is gorgeous," Jett added, then walked closer, trailing his fingers down her bare arm.

Jaydin remained in place, staring at her breasts.

"There'll be plenty of time to enjoy our woman's body. Right now we need to make another stand. We need to meet before the townspeople and officially accept Angus's challenge," Jaydin told them. Jeremiah wrapped his arm around her midsection, cupping her breast in the process.

She gasped but did not pull away, and Jeremiah licked his lips.

"She already knows my touch." He nipped her neck where the bite mark remained.

"She will soon learn all of our scents and bodies. I get to bite her next," Jett stated as he reached out and caressed a finger from her lips down her chin, over the cleavage of her breasts between the light, sheer fabric and straight to her mound.

She turned sideways, gasping from the intimate touch, and Jeremiah pulled her hard against him.

"You accept your Alpha's touch. Denying will only cause you punishment," he warned her.

"We need to go. Take her hand and keep her close. The Fennigan Pack will try to take her back," Torch said.

"They can try but they will wind up dead. We're packing silver. They're still living decades in the past," Jeremiah stated as he tapped his waist where the gun sat.

"Did Centron arrive yet?" Jeremiah asked.

"No. He is staying in the States as precaution. We'll need a contact there to assist us in handling any issues that arise after this take over here," Jaydin replied.

"He would have loved to be here to see Salina like this. So compliant and defeated," Jeremiah whispered as he tilted her chin toward him and kissed her softly on the lips. He ran his hand down her side, caressing her breasts, rubbing a thumb along her nipple.

They chuckled.

"He sure would," Jaydin said as they started walking and Jaydin took her hand to pull her closer.

Salina pulled away from him and he grabbed her hand.

"Stay right next to me and do as I say," he warned as they exited the room and headed to the meeting area outside. Little did Fennigan Pack know that this was a trap, that they weren't going to fight fair, and taking out Angus first, would weaken the others.

* * * *

Salina felt her chest tighten. She feared for her mates, but also feared the power that Torque had. Something inside of her tingled with confidence though, and she thought about the woman who had appeared. The one called Charity. As she thought about her name while Jaydin held her hand and Jeremiah kept one on her waist, she sensed magic around the area. She stared straight ahead, acted as if she were under Torque's spell, but evaluated the situation. She was a great homicide detective because little details stood out to her. The glowing eyes in the darkness that surrounded the building they came from. The tall, full trees that almost formed a semicircle around a large open area. In them she spotted more glowing eyes, and her mind reached out to one of the men hiding there. She blocked Torque from hearing her thoughts as she used her powers explained to her by the goddesses as she slept.

"I'd hate to be down there in the center. These silver bullets are going to kill every single one of them. Venificus, Fagan, Fennigan, and Declan packs will all die here today. It's historic, and I'm on the right side of this battle. Torque is a wizard, and now Carbarone Pack have the woman."

The wolf inhaled as she passed by from below. Silver bullets? Ambush? Declan Pack, Fagan, Venificus, and Fennigan Packs would all die. It would indeed be a massacre.

She made sure she blocked her thoughts from Torque and tried to contact her mates. She thought she felt one of them. *Eagan, Delaney, Adrian? Brady, Quinn, Angus? Someone please hear me.* Why weren't they answering? *I have to do something.*

The thought came to her as she remembered her abilities as the goddesses taught her. She could indeed read minds, yet she could alter a person's thinking. It was a safeguard, a power bestowed upon her as an angel on earth to help those killers who wanted to repent, and indeed had other qualities important enough to assist mankind and supernatural. She could make them be good. She could turn criminals into good citizens, but only when the gods and goddesses approved.

So why not make these men, these warriors in the trees fight against Carbarone instead of the others?

"Keep her right here next to us. If one of them attacks, have the men fire upon the lot of them," Jaydin ordered.

She needed to do something now. She had to give her mates and their friends a fighting chance.

Salina closed her eyes and concentrated. She sought out the minds, the voices and thoughts of all those men, wolves who felt loyalty to Carbarone Pack and Torque.

"You are not fighting the right wolves. They use you, each of you, to do their dirty work. Fennigan Pack, Fagan, Declan, and Venificus

are your leaders. They stand behind you, alongside you in the fight to maintain justice and protect the existence of Weres in this world and beyond. I know, because I am an angel on earth."

She heard their simultaneous outburst of denial until she said she was an angel. But then Torque interrupted the moment as Angus and his brothers, along with about ten other men, emerged from the tree line.

"Do as I say, or you all will die a most horrible death. I am an enforcer, a warrior of good over evil. You pull those triggers and shoot my mates and their allies, and you all die."

Jeremiah pulled her back against his chest. His large palm lay across her skin where the thin, sheer fabric opened. In this position her breasts nearly emerged from the top, and he wedged his thigh between her legs, spreading them open.

* * * *

Angus spoke to his brothers through their mind links.

"Remain calm. We know that there are wolves in the trees. The others will take them out. Do as we planned. Adrian, you head straight for our mate," Angus stated.

"You bet. But what the fuck is she wearing?" Adrian asked as he growled low.

"I can see her nipples from here and her pussy," Delaney said in anger.

Just then they watched Jeremiah lick along her neck as he cupped one of her breasts. She gasped, and Angus felt his own wolf surface.

"Release our mate now, Jaydin, and perhaps we'll let you live," Angus said.

"I think not, Angus. She is ours now. The sooner I kill you and your men, and finalize this takeover, the sooner I get to partake in her luscious body." Jaydin reached over, pressed his palm over her mound beneath her dress, and stroked her.

Salina gasped and tried to pull away, which only angered Angus's beast even more, but he couldn't react. Not even when Jaydin rubbed his hands along her mound and licked her neck.

"I am going to rip that fucking wolf's throat out. Let me do it now, Angus," Delaney stated through their mind link.

Salina moaned and then they heard her voice in their heads.

"Silver, trap, trees."

"Salina?" Adrian called out her name in his mind.

Angus felt her and then the power weakened. He looked up and saw Torque placing his hand on her shoulder. Her eyes were closed and her hands fell by her side.

"Enough talking. Do you challenge Jaydin Carbarone to a fight as Alpha to this territory, and all parcels of land across the United States that now belong to him?" Torque asked.

"I do."

"Then let's do it," Jaydin said.

Angus watched as Jaydin turned toward Salina, pulled her into his arms, and kissed her deeply. It nearly caused him to jump toward the man and kill him, but a process was in the works. His other men, warriors, were in position behind the men in the trees. They could take them out, and hopefully before Carbarone's army were able to use the silver bullets.

He was amazed at his mate's ability to try and help them even when under the wizard's spell.

"He dies next," Brady stated about Torque.

"Let's begin. Angus against Jaydin," Vargon Carbarone announced, and Angus received good wishes and luck from his friends and brothers as they formed a circle around the perimeter.

Angus looked at Salina, who seemed sedated and weak now. Jeremiah was running his hands all over her body. He licked her neck, and from here Angus could see the bite mark.

"I've waited a long time for this, Angus. It will be my pleasure to watch you die."

Angus looked at Jaydin as he circled him.

"I think not. It is you who will die tonight, Jaydin, then your brothers and that piece of shit wizard you took up with."

Jaydin swatted at Angus and the fight began. Round and round they started fighting as men using fists and their anger, but then Jaydin shifted midair and scraped his claw along Angus's shoulder, causing Angus to roar in pain and then shift to his wolf form.

Angus's wolf was dark brown, where Jaydin's was jet black.

They growled and bit at one another until Jaydin went low and Angus went high, clawing across Jaydin's chest. In a flash Jaydin howled, Torque yelled a command, and suddenly the circle lit up with fighting everywhere. Angus sensed the men falling from the trees, heard gunshots and wolves cry out in pain from getting hit with silver. He knew his brothers were okay, and then he sensed Adrian lunge toward the crowd of beasts to get to Salina.

The sound of her cries enraged his beast as Angus locked gazes with Jaydin's black eyes. "It's over, Carbarone. Salina belongs to Fennigan Pack, just as this land does."

He growled loudly. Smelling his mate's scent on Jaydin sent him over the edge, and he went for his jugular. He ripped out Jaydin's throat. As he spit it from his mouth, he turned, only to be attacked by another wolf. One after the next he pounded away, tore wolves' flesh, pulled out their hearts, bit into their throats. His determination and goal was to reach Salina before they could harm her more.

* * * *

Vargon Carbarone ran from the scene. Jeremiah and Jett held on to Salina until Adrian and Brady emerged. Adrian grabbed for Jeremiah as Brady attacked Jett, leaving Salina standing there on her own. Torque pulled her to him.

"Things have changed. You're coming with me." He dragged her from the scene.

Adrian called to his brothers through their link as he fought Jeremiah. They all shifted to their wolf forms and their own battles began. Adrian knew that Jeremiah was a dangerous, dirty-fighting wolf. But he was the one who bit their mate. He tried to force her to mate with him and his brothers and that in itself was his death sentence.

Round and round they fought one another with vigor and hatred. A few swipes from Jeremiah's paws and claws sent Adrian into an angry rage. Brady was no different as they simultaneously jumped onto their opponents and ripped their throats out.

"Torque has Salina. Find them!" Angus roared as the others continued to fight off the Carbarone army.

Brady, Delaney, Eagan, and Quinn headed into the house. They followed Salina's scent and could hear her screams. Angus and Adrian followed, trying to keep up and find them.

Her scent became so distant, so weak they thought they had lost her.

"No! No, damn you, she is our mate. She belongs to Fennigan!" Adrian roared in anger.

"I am here. Torque has an escape plan. I'm not going to go with him. I love you all, and he must not succeed," Salina said.

"No. No, you wait and we fight him. We can't lose you, Salina!" Angus said.

"Where are you?" Adrian asked. *"Tell us and we can help."*

"Salina, answer us. Answer your Alphas," Brady ordered.

There was nothing but silence and then Salina's agonizing scream as if she were in immense pain.

"No! Not again. Not Salina, too!" Delaney yelled.

* * * *

"You dare try to fight my control? I am more powerful than you. More powerful than any wizard."

Salina was lying on the ground. Torque had struck her repeatedly the moment he read her mind and heard her conversing with her mates, causing her to scream in pain.

"What's the plan now?" one of the guards asked Torque. There were six with them. All armed and ready.

Torque pulled her up by her hair. "We have a backup plan. Just follow me. I'd hate to have unexpected guests impede my plans."

His hold was firm on her arm, and Salina could feel her own temper rising, and the desire to fight, to rip this man apart, filled her heart and soul. But then came a calming sensation, that black coat of armor that seemed to prevent Torque from hearing her thoughts.

She saw the vision in her mind, and then sent a plan to Angus. She quickly let her mind recede under Torque's control just as they came to another door beyond the small tunnel they traveled through.

He nodded toward two of the Were men. "You go first. Make sure it's all clear. You two, run ahead and see of the car is waiting."

The last two remained with her and Torque.

She watched the four men exit first. There wasn't a sound. It was eerie, and trepidation filled her body.

Then they heard branches snapping. Torque pulled her closer, and peered out toward the darkness.

"Something is wrong," one of the other wolves stated.

"You think?" Torque asked sarcastically.

Salina felt her powers building stronger. She sensed what was right to do.

"Get ready to shoot up that entire area. Kill them all. Use the silver bullets," he said.

Fear grasped her insides as Torque pulled her closer to whisper against her lips. She scrunched her teeth together and tried pulling away, but he wouldn't have it.

"When I mark you, there won't be any way for them to help you. The marking of a wizard is more powerful than that of a wolf."

He licked across her mouth and she shook her head. He yanked her hard.

"Cooperate, and I'll wait until we're alone in bed before I bind myself to you."

"Go to hell. I belong to Fennigan Pack." Just as she said the words, deep growls and horrifying squeals of pain filled the night air.

The two guards shot their weapons into the night, and she reached for Torque's gun as wolves emerged from the forest line.

It was a moment of truth, chaos, and a split decision that could change everyone's destiny, especially Salina's.

She felt her eyes change as she battled for the weapon with Torque. Fangs drew sharp from her mouth. Her eyes burned and Torque's widened in shock. He came toward her, ready to bite into her, but Salina pulled the trigger and shoved him from her with such force he fell backward.

Before she could see if shooting him worked, he shifted into some monstrous-looking beast. In a flash one wolf, large, dark brown, flew through the air, gashing the beast's throat with its paw. Then there was a second wolf. He bit at the beast, tearing its flesh by its shoulder. A third one followed, then a forth, a fifth, and finally the sixth wolf stood atop the beast and tore its heart from its chest. It howled at the top of its lungs and the sound of more wolves howling along with the one wolf echoed through the night.

Salina tried to calm her breathing as the wolves transformed into her mates. Fennigan Pack had saved her.

"You didn't obey your Alphas," Brady reprimanded. He and his brothers stood side by side, all wearing only pants except for Adrian, who wore his kilt.

Salina stood up, watched them absorb her attire, and felt the love encompassing them all.

"Damn it, Salina, we could have lost you. Torque was prepared to kill you. I will not stand by and allow my mate, *our* mate, to disobey a direct order meant to protect you." Angus raged on. She stared at him, all muscles, dominance, and Alpha male. She felt her lip curl up, and an overwhelming urge came over her at his outburst. She stepped toward Angus and could see out of the corner of her eye that the others were just as angry but also intrigued by what she was going to do.

She shocked Angus as she jumped up into his arms, straddled his waist, wedged her breasts nearly to his chin, and held on to him. Staring down into his eyes and shocked expression, she gave him an order. "Just kiss me, Angus. The punishments can come later."

Before he could react, Salina covered his mouth and kissed him deeply, until her Alpha and his brothers surrounded her in a group hug, sniffing and licking her skin, absorbing her scent and clarifying that she indeed was safe and back in their arms.

She looked at Angus. "I love you so damn much."

Then she looked at the others, at Adrian, Brady, Quinn, Delaney, and Eagan. "I love each of you. Can we please go home now?"

"We are home, Salina. We're the new Alphas to a hell of a lot of land, and there are bad guys to catch and an angel to help us enforce the laws of the land," Adrian said.

She took a deep breath and wondered if she could stay here in Ireland. Could she leave her home and her father, Reggie?

"We are one completely now, Salina. Your father is fine, Reggie is going to live, and the six of us are going to be spending the next several months in bed," Brady said.

"Months?"

"Months," they all chimed in through their mind link. Salina hugged Angus as he carried her from the center of the woods and back across the land.

* * * *

Angus felt proud as he carried their mate across the land and between the crowds of onlookers. These were their people now, too.

Angus, his brothers, and Salina would help to build up their new territory along with Skylar Pack. Merging together would form another strategic front against any evil rogue supernaturals with convoluted ideas about taking over. Not on their watch.

"So this is the lovely Salina 'Sal' Santos? It is a pleasure to meet you."

"Salina, meet Vanderlan."

As Vanderlan bowed his head and then took her hand and kissed the top of it, Salina smiled.

The others moved in behind Vanderlan. There were Van, Miele, Randolph, Bently, and Baher. Angus introduced them all, and then came Dani.

"Meet our mate, Dani," Van said as he held her around the waist.

Salina tapped Angus's arm. "Set me down, please."

He gave her an expression in warning, and she smiled.

"Please, Alpha," she said, and the others all chuckled.

He set her down and Salina looked at Dani.

Dani smiled as she took her hand. "It is a pleasure to meet you, Salina. I see now why the gods and goddesses have chosen you. We are going to be very good friends." Dani pulled Salina into a hug and Salina smiled as she glanced at Angus.

When the women parted, Task Force Three approached and Delaney introduced Salina to William, Mick, Sean, Pat, and Kyle Declan. Then Eagan introduced her to Ava.

"It is an honor to meet you, Ava. Thank you all for your help," Salina said.

Ava smiled as Quinn placed his arm around Salina's waist and nuzzled against her neck.

"The pleasure is ours. We will meet and talk in a few days. In the meanwhile, your father and Reggie are safe at my castle," Ava told her.

"We may be a bit longer than a few days, Ava. There are some serious matters we need to work out," Brady said in a firm voice.

"Serious matters?" Salina asked.

Angus chuckled.

Adrian pulled Salina up into his arms and began to walk away with her.

"It may be months," he called over his shoulder.

"Salina, don't let them keep you too long. You all have work to do," she teased.

"Thank you all, we'll make it to the castle eventually," Angus said and winked at the men. They all headed out, following Adrian toward the building where they could be alone with their mate.

Angus smiled as he heard William speak to Ava.

"You know they're going to be alone in that house for quite some time?"

"Of course, William. If Fennigan Pack are anything like you guys, we won't be seeing them any time soon." The others laughed.

"I do recall our mate not being too concerned over that when we were in a bit of a battle ourselves," Mick reminded her.

"We'd better make sure the servants are on call and have plenty of food sent over. Sealing the mating bond takes a lot out of a woman," she teased.

Angus looked back as Sean, Kyle, and Pat stared at Ava intently.

"The bond always needs work, mate. How about we head back to the castle and reminisce?" Sean said, pulling Ava into his arms and kissing her.

Angus chuckled and joined his brothers and mate inside the building. He was definitely going to ensure that the bond was secure and thoroughly love his mate. He heard Salina squeal and then laugh. His wolf grew impatient and needy as he ran up the stairs in hot pursuit of their woman.

* * * *

Salina was breathing heavy as she continued backstepping until her ass and back hit the wall behind her.

Her men, all six of them, were stripping. The sight of their perfect, muscular bodies gave her palpitations. She gasped at the sight of their thick, hard cocks. All of them were stroking them, staring at her with hungry eyes.

"That fucking outfit is going to get burned," Brady stated as he eyed her over. "Every wolf could see what's ours."

"Every inch of hers is ours, and if another wolf comes sniffing, I'll rip his heart out," Quinn said.

Angus growled low, his eyes glowing, his chest heaving up and down, and she gasped when he reach up, his hand half human, half wolf, with claws. In a flash the material fell from her body, revealing her skin, her every curve adorned in jewelry.

"Get ready, lassie, we are all going to make love to you and get rid of the scent of every other wolf that came too close."

She nibbled her bottom lip, a bit overwhelmed with his aggressiveness.

"No need to worry, I guarantee it will be quite pleasurable," Delaney said as she watched the others lick their lips and eye her over. Her pussy clenched. She closed her eyes and moaned. They hadn't even actually, physically touched her yet, and she already creamed herself.

They sniffed the air.

Salina closed her eyes and smiled as Angus cupped her breasts and her mates began to spread scattered kisses along her skin.

"Ours," Eagan whispered.

"Ours," Delaney added.

"Ours," Quinn said, pulling her away from the wall and in the center between them. She was overwhelmed with love, desire, and hunger for her mates.

"All of yours. Now make love to me. I need each of you, too," Salina said and Angus shook his head and made a "tsk, tsk" noise with his mouth.

"Someone needs to learn who's in charge."

She locked gazes with his stern expression and deep blue, almost gray eyes right before he lifted her up and placed her on the bed on her belly. His big strong hands gripped her hips, pulled her ass and pussy over the edge, and thrust a finger into her cunt.

Salina widened her stance and cried out as the first smack hit her ass.

"Ours," Brady stated.

A smack, a caress, and then a thrust of fingers, and she was already coming hard. When she felt the kisses to her back and her ass then large hands caress up her thighs soothing her, arousing her, she couldn't take it any longer.

Salina hopped up on all fours, stuck her ass out and looked over her shoulder.

"I desperately need all of you right now. Stop teasing me and just make love to me already." She saw their angry expressions and knew they probably were serious about being in charge all the time. So she knew it was one of those times that she needed to tone down her independent, take-charge attitude and let her men have all the control.

She gave a pouty face and then reached underneath her to her cunt where her fingers collided with Angus's.

"I need you all so badly. Fuck me, pretty please," she teased.

"Holy fuck." In a New York second, Brady was underneath her, aligning his cock with her pussy and thrusting upward. She gasped at the instant feeling of being filled. Plus, she felt so wild and needy it made her growl for more.

Behind her she felt a moist, wet tongue stroke back and forth against her anus. *Angus.*

His hands gripped her hips and he licked along her neck, nibbled against her skin near the bite from Jeremiah.

His growl made her nipples tingle and her pussy pulsate.

"Take it all away, Angus. Cover me with your scent. Mark me your mate again and again. Do it, baby," she encouraged.

He gripped her hair and she turned sideways to look up at him. "Get ready, Salina, it's time you learned what life is going to be like being the mate to Fennigan Pack."

She was so aroused, so excited that when he pressed his cock between her ass cheeks and against her puckered hole, she shoved back to get him inside faster.

It earned her a smack and then two cocks thrust into her together. As she moaned and gasped, trying to get used to the deep, penetrating strokes from Angus and Brady, Quinn touched her cheek and she opened her eyes to see him stroking his cock.

"Get that mouth over here, woman. Your men want to fuck you in every hole. We own them all, now."

Greedily, she opened for his cock, licking along the tip and base before she took as much of him down her throat as possible.

She felt so wild and out of control her body erupted in another orgasm.

"Fuck!" Brady yelled out, thrusting upward and exploding inside of her. He pulled her down as Angus pressed her back lower and Brady bit into her shoulder over Jeremiah's mark. She felt Quinn grow thicker and then shoot his seed down her throat. She swallowed his cum as quickly as she could, her body winding up tight again. He thrust two more times, biting into her shoulder. She released his cock and moaned, gasping for air, but then her focus was on Quinn moving to the side, and Angus stroking his cock faster, deeper into her ass.

"Mine. You are mine for eternity mate." Angus came inside of her, roared, and then bit into her shoulder near Brady's mark, over Jeremiah's.

They caressed her skin and her hair, and Brady cupped her cheeks and stared at her. "I love you, mate. Never leave us again. You hear?" he asked, sounding so emotional. But before she could analyze his words and determine if those were tears in his eyes or not, he covered her mouth and kissed her deeply.

She had little reprieve as she felt Angus slowly pull from her ass, caressing the cheeks and kissing along her back.

Brady gently pulled away from her mouth. "The others need you now, too."

"As I need them," she said, and he winked.

A strong arm wrapped around her midsection and a hand cupped her breast.

Delaney.

Adrian scooted into Brady's spot and locked gazes with Salina.

"I got a nice hard cock for that sweet little cunt, lassie. Come on down here and ride your mate," he said and winked.

She licked her lips and then gasped as Delaney pinched her nipple.

"Round two is about to start." Delaney placed her onto Adrian, who pulled her down quickly for a deep, sensual kiss as Delaney caressed her ass. The bed dipped, and she knew that Eagan was there. She was going to have cock in every hole once again.

How the hell am I going to get used to making love to six men like this?

"Practice makes perfect mate," Adrian said through their mind link as he aligned his cock with her pussy and thrust upward.

The others chuckled, and with a quick glance to the left, she saw Quinn, Angus, and Brady watching as her other lovers prepared her body for round two.

Delaney caressed her ass and began to lick back and forth across her puckered hole. His hands felt odd for a moment and then he growled before pressing what felt like a very thick, long tongue firmer against her puckered hole.

"Oh God, Delaney, what are you doing? What is that?" she asked.

Eagan caressed Salina's hair, drawing her attention to him and his cock as Adrian thrust upward and played with her beasts. It was sensation overload.

Her eyes locked on Eagan's blue ones. "Wolves have really talented tongues."

Just thinking that Delaney was using his long, thick, wolfen tongue to get her ass ready for his cock inspired her thoughts.

Ooh, how would it feel pressed up into my pussy, hitting that special spot?

As she finished the thought, Adrian lifted up, separating their bodies. She was about to reprimand him until she felt Delaney's wolf tongue plunge up into her pussy. Over and over again he thrust it into her and she screamed as her body convulsed.

The men chuckled and before she could get upset or even think of some witty verbal response, Adrian was back inside of her and Delaney's cock thrust into her anus in smooth, even strokes. She was breathless, completely out of control, and feeling like a rag doll between them when Eagan pulled her toward his cock. She opened for him and he pressed inside of her, grunting about not being able to last.

In and out they worked in sync, fucking her in every hole, caressing her body, pinching her nipples, and nibbling her skin. When she felt Delaney's hands turn to claws against her hip bones, she knew she was going to come.

Delaney's claws skimmed along her ass cheeks where his cock was lost inside of her and then over her hip bones to the top of her mound, giving her chills of excitement. He tapped the claws against her pussy lips while Adrian pumped up into her harder, faster. Then Eagan came, shooting his seed down her throat, and bit into her shoulder. She could hardly lick him clean in this position, but she hungrily ate at his cock. When she released Eagan's cock to breathe, Delaney was still using his claws and Adrian was gripping her so tight and rocking up and down she lost it and screamed out in ecstasy.

Delaney exploded inside of her next and then bit into her shoulder. She felt the magic swirl around her. For each time they bit her something changed inside of her. Something grew even stronger.

Delany caressed her ass and then slowly pulled from her body. With little effort and complete dominance, Adrian rolled her to her back and pulled her slightly off the bed. He gripped her hands and held them above her head, exposing her breasts to his mouth. He rapidly gyrated his hips, trusting, stroking deeply and making her nearly lose focus. He was so dominant and wild.

"Fuck, lassie, I'm coming. Come with me now. Come," he ordered, but he must have sensed her body tighten, not quite ready to come. He released her hands and maneuvered his hand below them to find her puckered hole.

She gasped and he pressed his digit into her anus while he used his cock to thrust into her pussy.

"Come for him now," Angus ordered. The others gathered around them, waiting for Adrian and her to come and for Adrian to bite her, brought on a surge of desire.

"Harder, Adrian. Fuck me harder," she told him.

He pulled his finger from her anus and grabbed her hips. She felt the claws against her skin as he pumped into her, his eyes glowing, his muscles glossed with perspiration, and his intricate tattoos sending her over the edge.

"Yes!" She shook with a massive orgasm. Adrian roared. He actually roared and it echoed through the room then straight to her soul. He then bit into her neck and she hugged him to her. His tongue licking and sealing the wound made her feel content and sated.

"Holy shit, life doesn't get any better than this," Adrian said.

She looked at him as he lifted up and kissed her sweetly before he pulled from her body.

She closed her eyes, not even caring that she lay there naked, marked, and thoroughly fucked by her men.

"Don't you dare fall asleep, lassie. We've got plans for you," Quinn challenged, climbing up between her legs and then using his thumbs to tweak her nipples.

She opened her eyes and felt a sense of belonging, completion, and love.

"I wasn't falling asleep. I was waiting on you. Are you sure you're ready to do it again?" she challenged. Quinn gave her a firm expression as he tapped the tip of his very hard cock against her pussy lips.

"Pretty tough talk for a human. You sure you can handle us wolves?" he asked.

"Oh, I can handle all of you, but remember, I'm not only human."

Quinn reached up and caressed her cheek. "Our own Earth Angel, to love, protect, and enjoy." He thrust the tip of his cock slightly into the opening of her pussy.

"And some other things, too," she teased. "But we'll get to that later. We have all the time in the world, remember?"

"What other things?" Angus asked as he, Delaney, Eagan, Brady, and Adrian joined her and Quinn on the bed.

She closed her eyes and let them read her mind. She let them see all she had learned during the time she was held captive by Carbarone and Torque.

"When Jeremiah bit into my skin, he somehow gave me some of his abilities as Were and vampire. Not that I can shift into these things, or at least I don't think so. It's more like weapons, tools to deal with the battles yet to come and my mission on earth as an angel of the law. You six Alphas will stand beside me, my equals, as we enforce the laws and bring justice to all victims and their families."

"Your equals?" Angus asked, and she felt the others feeling the same thing. This was hard for them. They were Alpha wolves and warriors.

"In most areas," she teased and then caressed Quinn's chest, moving further down until she held his cock in her hand. *"But how*

about you six can be in charge, most of the time in the bedroom?" She started spreading her thighs and pushing Quinn's cock up into her cunt.

He grabbed her wrists and pressed them up above her head, locking her in place.

She gasped at his strength and control, and of course her pussy leaked, indicating she liked being ordered around by her Alphas.

"How about always equals, everywhere, mate," Quinn said. The others joined him, kissing and suckling her skin, pinching her nipples, getting her body ready for more cock. And she loved every second of it. Relinquished complete control to her six sexy Irish Alphas, whose brogues alone could make her give in to any of their sexual demands.

"That's good to know, lassie. 'Cause we're gonna love using our brogues and our Alpha attitudes to make you putty in our hands," Adrian whispered against her neck. She shivered and barely got out any words as her men prepared her body for more.

"Bring it on, laddie," she said in her own version of an Irish brogue, just as Quinn thrust up into her cunt, sending her body skyrocketing to another world.

"By the gods, I love Ireland," she said.

"And Ireland loves you," Angus added.

THE END

WWW.DIXIELYNNDWYER.COM

ABOUT THE AUTHOR

People seem to be more interested in my name than where I get my ideas for my stories from. So I might as well share the story behind my name with all my readers.

My momma was born and raised in New Orleans. At the age of twenty, she met and fell in love with an. Needless to say, the family was a bit taken aback by this as they hoped she would marry a family friend. It was a modern day arranged marriage kind of thing and my momma downright refused.

Being that my momma's families were descendants of the original English speaking Southerners, they wanted the family blood line to stay pure. They were wealthy and my father's family was poor.

Despite attempts by my grandpapa to make my father leave and destroy the love between them, my parents married. They recently celebrated their sixtieth wedding anniversary.

I am one of six children born to my parents. I am a combination of both Irish and a true Southern belle. With a name like Dixie Lynn Dwyer it's no wonder why people are curious about my name.

Just as my parents had a love story of their own, I grew up intrigued by the lifestyles of others. My imagination as well as my need to stray from the straight and narrow made me into the woman I am today.

For all titles by Dixie Lynn Dwyer, please visit
www.bookstrand.com/dixie-lynn-dwyer

Siren Publishing, Inc.
www.SirenPublishing.com

CPSIA information can be obtained
at www.ICGtesting.com
Printed in the USA
LVOW01s0102310116

472963LV00021B/283/P